Jean de La Fontaine

Tales and Novels in Verse

Vol. 1

Jean de La Fontaine

Tales and Novels in Verse
Vol. 1

ISBN/EAN: 9783337393779

Printed in Europe, USA, Canada, Australia, Japan

Cover: Foto ©Andreas Hilbeck / pixelio.de

More available books at **www.hansebooks.com**

TALES AND NOVELS

IN VERSE

BY

J. DE LA FONTAINE

WITH EIGHTY-FIVE ENGRAVINGS BY

EISEN

AND THIRTY-EIGHT AFTER

LANCRET, BOUCHER, PATER, Etc.

IN TWO VOLUMES

VOLUME THE FIRST

LONDON: PRIVATELY PRINTED FOR
THE SOCIETY OF ENGLISH BIBLIOPHILISTS
MDCCCXCVI

INTRODUCTORY MEMOIR

JEAN DE LA FONTAINE was born in the year 1621, at Château Thierry, where his family held a good position. After receiving an imperfect education at home and at Rheims, the young La Fontaine, at the age of twenty, entered the Seminary of the Oratorians, but left it in eighteen months to lead an idle and irregular life at home.

It is said that his native talent was first roused by the recitation of an ode of Malherbe, and, pursuing his poetical studies, he acquired knowledge of the great writers of classical times, reading Homer, Plato, Virgil, Horace, in addition to the two authors who perhaps influenced him more directly—Terence and Phædrus. The works of Rabelais and Boccaccio furnished him with materials and suggestions for many of his stories, and he borrowed largely from them.

At the age of twenty-six, in compliance with the wishes of his family, he married, and succeeded to his father's appointment; but the marriage was not a happy one, and his eccentric temperament was hardly consistent with the proper performance of his official duties. Seven years later, after publishing at Rheims a translation of the Eunuchus *of Terence — a work of no particular interest—he went to Paris, where he lived for several years under the protection of Fouquet, the Mæcenas of the time. Upon the fall of his patron he was placed in a difficult position. The* Grand Monarque *was displeased with his irregular life, and withstood all the poet's efforts to obtain the patronage of the Court. However, by the kindness of two ladies, he was rescued from absolute want, and in* 1665 *brought out the first series of his* Contes, *the work being completed at intervals during the next ten years. During this period he produced, in addition to his* Contes, Psyche, *a mythological novel;* Adonis, *a narrative poem, and the first six books of the* Fables. *These latter were not completed till more than twenty years later, when the poet was seventy-three years of age. In the interval his reputation had greatly increased, and in his later years he was maintained first by Mme. de la Sablière, and then by M. de Hervard, in whose house he died in the spring of the year* 1695. *He was buried in the cemetery of St. Joseph, by the side of Molière.*

His later works seem to show a reaction from the freedom of the writings of his early manhood, and the Fables *would seem wholly inconsistent with the* Contes, *if we were ignorant that in his later years La Fontaine seemed to turn once more to the religion with which he had been connected in his youth, and that he died, strange as it may seem, a grave, sincere penitent.*

In addition to the works above mentioned, La Fontaine was the author of several comedies, two operas, and many poems of varying excellence and importance. The Contes, *translated in the present volume, are original only in their treatment and expression. Gathered from all sources, they gain uniformity from the delicacy with which they are handled, and from the skill with which they are adapted to the form required by the author. No better indication of their popularity and of their correspondence with the tastes of the time can be given than the elaborate illustrations with which they were embellished.*

The beautiful series of small plates designed for the book by the celebrated Eisen, which will be found in the present edition, are sufficient proofs of this. At the same time, the Contes *furnished appropriate subjects for Boucher, the President of the Academy; for Lancret the imitator, and for Pater the pupil of Watteau, and for other famous artists of the time ; and their pictures, engraved of a uniform size, will also be found in these volumes. Perhaps at no other period in the history of art could such a number of men of talent be found who were suited in every way to illustrate the graceful license of the* Contes *of La Fontaine.*

THE AUTHOR'S PREFACE

TO THE FIRST VOLUME OF THESE WORKS

I HAD resolved not to consent to the printing of these Tales until I had joined to them those of Boccaccio, which are those most to my taste; but several persons have advised me to produce at once what I have remaining of these trifles, in order that the curiosity to see them, which is still in its first ardour, may not grow cold. I give way to this advice without much difficulty, and I have thought well to profit by the occasion. Not only can I do so, but it would be vanity on my part to despise such an advantage. It is enough for me to wish that no one should be imposed upon in my favour, and to follow a road contrary to that of certain persons, who only make friends in order to gain voices in their favour by their means; creatures of the Cabal, very different from that Spaniard who prided himself on being the son of his own works. Although I may still be as much in want of these artifices as any other person, I cannot decide to employ them; however, I shall accom-

*modate myself, if possible, to the taste of the times, in-
structed as I am by my own experience that there is
nothing which is more necessary. Indeed, one cannot
say that all seasons are suitable for all classes of books.
We have seen the Roundelays, the Metamorphoses, the
Crambos, reign one after another. At present these
gallantries are out of date, and nobody cares about them :
so certain is it that what pleases at one time may not
please at another ! Only works of truly solid merit and
sovereign beauty are well received by all minds and in
all ages, without possessing any other passport than the
sole merit with which they are filled. As mine are so
far distant from such a high degree of perfection, prudence
advises that I should keep them in my cabinet unless I
choose well my own time for producing them. This is
what I have done, or what I have tried to do, in this
edition, in which I have only added new tales, because
it seemed to me that people were prepared to take pleasure
in them. There are some which I have extended, and
others which I have abridged, only for the sake of diver-
sifying them and making them less tedious. But I am
occupying myself with matters about which perhaps people
will take no notice, whilst I have reason to apprehend
much more important objections. Two only of any weight
can be made against me: the one, that this book is
licentious; the other, that it does not sufficiently spare the
fair sex. With regard to the first, I say boldly that the
nature of what is understood as a tale decides what
it shall be, it being an indispensable law, according
to Horace, or rather according to reason and common*

sense, that one must conform to the nature of the things about which one writes. Now, that I should be permitted to write thus, as so many others have done, and with success, cannot, I think, be doubted, and people cannot condemn me for so doing without also condemning Ariosto before me and the ancients before Ariosto. It may be said that I should have done better to have suppressed certain details, or at least to have disguised them. Nothing was more easy, but it would have weakened the tale and taken away some of its charm. So much circumspection is necessary only in works which promise great discretion from the beginning, either by their subject or by the manner in which they are treated. I confess that it is necessary to keep within certain limits, and that the narrowest are the best; also it must be allowed that to be too scrupulous would spoil all. Any man who tried to make Boccaccio as modest as Virgil would assuredly produce nothing worth having, and would sin against the laws of propriety by setting himself the task to observe them; for, to speak correctly, in matters of verse and prose extreme modesty and propriety are two very different things. Cicero makes the latter consist in saying what it is appropriate that one should say, considering the place, the time, and the persons to whom one is speaking. This principle once admitted, it is not a fault of judgment to entertain the people of to-day with tales which are a little broad. Nor in this do I sin against morality. If there is anything in my writings which is capable of making an impression on the mind, it is by no means the gaiety of these Tales; it passes off lightly. I should rather fear a tranquil melancholy, into which the most chaste and modest novels are very capable of plunging us, and which is a great preparation for love. As to the second objection, by which people reproach me that this book does wrong to womankind, they would be right if I were speaking seriously; but who does not see that this is all in jest, and consequently cannot injure? We must not be afraid on that account that marriages in the future will be less frequent, and husbands more on their guard. It may still be objected that these Tales are unfounded, or that they have everywhere a foundation easy to destroy; in short, that there are absurdities and not the least tinge of probability. I reply in a few words that I have my authorities; and, besides, it is neither truth nor probability which makes the beauty and the charm of these Tales; it is only the manner of telling them. These are the principal points on which I have thought it necessary to defend myself. I leave the rest to the censors; the more so as it would be an infinite undertaking to pretend to reply to all. Criticism never stops short, nor ever lacks subjects on which to exercise herself; even if those which I am able to foresee were taken from her, she would soon discover others.

CONTENTS

VOLUME THE FIRST

CONTENTS

LIST OF ENGRAVINGS

ON COPPER

VOLUME THE FIRST

TALES AND NOVELS

OF

J. DE LA FONTAINE

JOCONDE

IN Lombardy's fair land, in days of yore,
  A prince possessed of youthful charms a store;
    Each fair, with anxious look, his favours sought,
And every heart within his net was caught.
Quite proud of beauteous form and smart address,
In which the world was led to acquiesce,
He cried one day, while all attention paid,
"I'll bet a million Nature never made,
Beneath the sun, another man like me,
Whose symmetry with mine can well agree.
If such exist, and here will come, I swear
I'll show him every lib'ral princely care."

  A noble Roman, who the challenge heard,
This answer gave the king his soul preferred:

                                                       A

"Great prince, if you would see a handsome man,
To have my brother here should be your plan.
A frame more perfect Nature never gave;
But this to prove, your courtly dames I crave
May judge the fact, when I'm convinced they'll find,
Like you, the youth will please all womankind;
And since so many sweets at once may cloy,
'Twere well to have a partner in your joy."

The king, surprised, expressed a wish to view
This brother, formed on lines so very true.
"We'll see," said he, "if here his charms divine
Attract the heart of every nymph, like mine;
And should success attend our am'rous lord,
To you, my friend, full credit we'll accord."

Away the Roman flew Joconde to get
(So named was he in whom these features met);
'Midst woods and lawns, retired from city strife,
And lately wedded to a beauteous wife.
If blessed I know not; but with such a fair,
On him must rest the folly to despair.

The Roman courtier came, his business told;
The brilliant offers from the monarch bold.
His mission had success, but still the youth
Distraction felt, which 'gan to shake his truth.
A pow'rful monarch's favour *there* he viewed;
A partner *here*, with melting tears bedewed;
And while he wavered on the painful choice,
She thus addressed her spouse with plaintive voice:

"Can you, Joconde, so truly cruel prove,
To quit my fervent love in courts to move ?
The promises of kings are airy dreams,
And scarcely last beyond the day's extremes ;
By watchful, anxious care alone retained,
And lost, through mere caprice, as soon as gained.
If weary of my charms, alas ! you feel,
Still think, my love, what joys these woods conceal.
Here dwell around tranquillity and ease ;
The streams' soft murmurs and the balmy breeze
Invite to sleep ; these vales where breathe the doves,
All, all, my dear Joconde, renew our loves.
You laugh !   Ah! cruel, go, expose thy charms ;
Grim death will quickly spare me these alarms !"

Joconde's reply our records ne'er relate,
Nor what he did, nor how he left his mate ;
And since contemp'raries decline the task,
'Twere folly such details of me to ask.
We're told, howe'er, when ready to depart,
With flowing tears she pressed him to her heart ;
And on his arm a brilliant bracelet placed,
With hair around her picture nicely traced.
"This guard in full remembrance of my love,"
She cried ; then clasped her hands to powers above.

To see such dire distress and poignant grief
Might lead to think soon death would bring relief ;
But I, who know full well the female mind,
At best oft doubt affliction of the kind.

Joconde set out at length ; but that same morn,
As on he moved, his soul with anguish torn,

He found the picture he had quite forgot,
Then turned his steed, and back began to trot.
While musing what excuse to make his mate,
At home he soon arrived, and oped the gate,
Alighted unobserved, ran up the stairs,
And ent'ring to the lady unawares,
He found this darling rib, so full of charms,
Entwined within a valet's brawny arms!

'Midst first emotions of the husband's ire,
To stab them while asleep he felt desire.
Howe'er, he nothing did;—the courteous wight,
In this dilemma, clearly acted right.
The less of such misfortunes said is best;
'Twere well the soul of feeling to divest;
Their lives, through pity or prudential care,
With much reluctance he was led to spare.
Asleep he left the pair, for if awake,
In honour, he a diff'rent step would take.
"Had any smart gallant supplied my place,"
Said he, "I might put up with this disgrace;
But nought consoles the thought of such a beast.
Dan Cupid wantons, or is blind at least;
A bet, or some such whim, induced the god
To give his sanction to amours so odd."

This perfidy Joconde so much dismayed,
His spirits drooped, his lilies 'gan to fade;
No more he looked the charmer he had been;
And when the court's gay dames his face had seen,
They cried, "Is this the beauty we were told
Would captivate each heart, or young or old?

Why, he's the jaundice;—every view displays
The mien of one just fasted forty days!"

With secret pleasure this Astolphus learned;
The Roman, for his brother, risks discerned,
Whose secret griefs were carefully concealed
(And these Joconde could never wish revealed);
Yet, spite of gloomy looks and hollow eyes,
His graceful features pierced the wan disguise,
Which failed to please alone through want of life,
Destroyed by thinking on a guilty wife.

The God of Love, in pity to our swain,
At last revoked Black Care's corroding reign;
For, doubtless, in his views he oft was crossed,
While such a lover to the world was lost.

The hero of our tale at length, we find,
Was well rewarded: Love again proved kind;
For, musing as he walked alone one day,
And passed a gall'ry (held a secret way),
A voice in plaintive accents caught his ear,
And from the neighb'ring closet came, 'twas clear:
" My dear Curtade, my only hope below,
In vain I love;—you colder, colder grow,
While round no fair can boast so fine a face,
And numbers wish they might supply thy place;
Whilst thou with some gay page preferr'st a bet,
Or game at dice with some low, vulgar set,
To meeting me alone ; and when just now
To thee I sent, with rage thou knitt'st thy brow,

And Dorimene with every curse abused;—
Then played again, since better that amused,
And left me here, as if not worth a thought,
Or thou didst scorn what I so fondly sought."

Astonishment at once our Roman seized.
But who's the fair that thus her bosom eased ?
Or who's the gay Adonis formed to bless ?
You'd try a day and not the secret guess.
The queen's the belle;—and, doubtless you will stare,
The king's own dwarf the idol of her care!

The Roman saw a crevice in the wood,
Through which he took a peep from where he stood.
To Dorimene our lovers left the key,
Which she had dropt when lately forced to flee,
And this Joconde picked up—a lucky hit,
Since he could use it when he best thought fit.
"It seems," said he, "I'm not alone in *name ;*
And since a prince so handsome is the same,
Although a valet has supplied my place,
Yet see, the queen prefers a dwarf's embrace."

This thought consoled so well, his youthful rays
Returned, and e'en excelled his former days ;
And those who lately ridiculed his charms
Now anxious seemed to revel in his arms.
'Twas who could have him ; even prudes grew kind ;—
By many belles Astolphus was resigned ;
Though still the king retained enough, 'twas seen ;—
But now let us resume the dwarf and queen.

Our Roman, having satisfied his eyes,
At length withdrew, confounded by surprise.
Who follows courts must oft with care conceal,
And scarcely know what sight and ears reveal.

Yet by Joconde the king was loved so well,
What now he'd seen he greatly wished to tell ;
But since to princes full respect is due,
And what concerns them, howsoever true,
If thought displeasing, should not be disclosed
In terms direct, but obviously disposed,
To catch the mind, Joconde at ease detailed,
From days of yore to those he now bewailed,
The names of emp'rors and of kings whose brows,
By wily wives, were crowned with leafless boughs,
And who, without repining, viewed their lot,
Nor bad made worse, but thought things best forgot.
" E'en I, who now your Majesty address,"
Continued he, " am sorry to confess,
The very day I left my native earth,
To wait upon a prince of royal birth,
Was forced t' acknowledge cuckoldom among
The gods who rule the matrimonial throng,
And sacrifice thereto with aching heart :
Cornuted heads dire torments oft impart."

The tale he then detailed that raised his spleen,
And what within the closet he had seen.
The king replied, " I will not be so rude
To question what so clearly you have viewed ;
Yet, since 'twere better full belief to gain,
A glimpse of such a fact I should obtain.

Pray bring me thither."   Instantly our wight
Astolphus led, where both his ears and sight
Full proof received, which struck the prince with awe,
Who stood amazed at what he heard and saw.
But soon reflection's all-convincing power
Induced the king vexation to devour;
True courtier like, who dire misfortunes braves,
Feels sprouting horns, yet smiles at fools and knaves.
"Our wives," said he, "a pretty trick have played,
And shamefully the marriage-bed betrayed.
Let us the compliment return, my friend,
And round the country our amours extend;
But, in our plan the better to succeed,
Our names we'll change;—no servants we shall need.
For your relation I desire to pass,
So you'll true freedom use; then with a lass
We more at ease shall feel, more pleasure gain,
Than if attended by my usual train."

Joconde with joy the king's proposal heard;
On which the latter with his friend conferred.
Said he, "'Twere surely right to have a book,
In which to place the names of those we hook,
The whole arranged according to their rank,
And I'll engage no page remains a blank,
But ere we leave the range of our design,
E'en scrup'lous dames shall to our wish incline.
Our persons handsome, with engaging air,
And sprightly, brilliant wit no trifling share,—
'Twere strange, possessing such engaging charms,
They should not tumble freely in our arms."

The baggage ready, and the paper-book,
Our smart gallants the road together took.
But 'twould be vain to number their amours;
With beauties Cupid favoured them by scores;
Blessèd if only seen by either swain,
And doubly blessed who could attention gain.
Nor wife of alderman, nor wife of mayor,
Of justice, nor of governor, was there
Who did not anxiously desire her name
Might straight be entered in the *Book of Fame!*
Hearts which before were thought as cold as ice,
Now warmed at once and melted in a trice.

Some infidel, I fancy, in my ear
Would whisper, " Probabilities, I fear,
Are rather wanting to support the fact;
However perfectly gallants may act,
To gain a heart requires full many a day."
If more be requisite I cannot say;
'Tis not my plan to dupe or young or old,
But such to me, howe'er, the tale is told,
And Ariosto never truth forsakes;
Yet, if at every step a writer takes,
He's closely questioned as to time and place,
He ne'er can end his work with easy grace.
To those from whom just credence I receive,
Their tales I promise fully to believe.

At length, when our advent'rers round had played,
And danced with every widow, wife, and maid,
The full-blown lily and the tender rose,
Astolphus said, " Though clearly, I suppose,

We can as many hearts securely link
As e'er we like, yet better now, I think,
To stop a while in some delightful spot,
And that before satiety we've got;
For true it is, with love as with our meat,
If we variety of dishes eat,
The doctors tell us inj'ry will ensue,
And too much raking none can well pursue.
Let us some pleasing fair one then engage
To serve us both :—enough she'll prove, I'll wage."

    Joconde at once replied, "With all my heart,
And I a lady know who'll take the part;
She's beautiful, possesses store of wit,
And is the wife of one above a cit."

    "With such to meddle would be indiscreet,"
Replied the king.   "More charms we often meet
Beneath a chambermaid or laundress' dress
Than any rich coquette can well possess.
Besides, with those less form is oft required,
While dames of quality must be admired,
Their whims complied with, though suspicions rise,
And every hour produces fresh surprise.
But this sweet charmer of inferior birth
A treasure proves, a source of bliss on earth;
No trouble she to carry here nor there,
No balls she visits, and requires no care;
The conquest easy, we may talk or not.
The only difficulty we have got
Is how to find one we may faithful view;
So let us choose a girl to love quite new."

" Since these," replied the youth, "your thoughts appear,
What think you of our landlord's daughter here?
That she's a perfect virgin I've no doubt,
Nor can we find a chaster round about;
Her very doll more innocent won't prove
Than this sweet nymph designed with us to move."

The scheme our prince's approbation met:
" The very girl," said he, " I wished to get.
This night be our attack; and if her heart
Surrenders when our wishes we impart,
But one perplexity will then remain;—
'Tis who her virgin favours shall obtain.
The honour's all a whim, and I, as king,
At once assuredly should claim the thing.
The rest 'tis very easy to arrange;
As matters suit we presently can change."

" If *ceremony* 'twere," Joconde replied,
" All cavil then we quickly could decide;
Precedence would no doubt with you remain.
But this is quite another case, 'tis plain;
And equity demands that we agree
By lot to settle which the man shall be."

The noble youths no arguments would spare,
And each contended for the spoiler's care.
Howe'er, Joconde obtained the lucky hit,
And first embraced this fancied dainty bit.

The girl who was the noble rivals' aim
That evening to the room for something came.

Our heroes gave her instantly a chair,
And lavished praises on her face and hair ;
A diamond ring soon sparkled in her eyes ;
Its pleasing powers at sight obtained the prize.

The bargain made, she, in the dead of night,
When silence reigned and all was void of light,
With careful steps their anxious wish obeyed,
And 'tween them both she presently was laid.
'Twas Paradise, they thought, where all is nice,
And our young spark believed he broke the ice.

The folly I forgive him ;—'tis in vain
On this to reason, idle to complain ;
The wise have oft been duped, it is confest,
And Solomon, it seems, among the rest.
But gay Joconde felt nothing of the kind,
A secret pleasure glowed within his mind ;
He thought Astolphus wondrous bliss had missed,
And that himself alone the fair had kissed ;
A clod, howe'er, who lived within the place,
Had, prior to the Roman, her embrace.

The soft amour extended through the night ;
The girl was pleased, and all proceeded right.
The foll'wing night, the next, 'twas still the same.
Young Clod at length her coldness 'gan to blame ;
And as he felt suspicions of the act,
He watched her steps and verified the fact.
A quarrel instantly between them rose.
Howe'er, the fair, his anger to compose,

And favour not to lose, on honour vowed
That when the sparks were gone, and time allowed,
She would oblige his craving, fierce desire.
To which the village lad replied with ire:
" Pray what care I for any tavern guest
Of either sex ?—to *you* I now protest,
If I be not indulged this very night,
I'll publish your amours in mere despite."

" How can we manage it ? " replied the belle.
" I'm quite distressed ;—indeed, the truth to tell,
I've promised them this night to come again,
And if I fail, no doubt can then remain
But I shall lose the ring, their pledged reward,
Which would, you know, for *me* be very hard."

"To *you* I wish the ring," replied young Clod ;
" But do they sleep in bed, or only nod ?
Tell me, pray." "Oh," said she, "they sleep most sound.
But then between them placed shall I be found,
And while the one amidst love's frolics sports,
The other quiet lies, or Morpheus courts."
On hearing this the rustic lad proposed
To visit her when others' eyes were closed.
"Oh ! never risk it," quickly she replied ;
" 'Twere folly to attempt it by their side."
He answered, " Never fear, but only leave
The door ajar, and me they'll not perceive."

The door she left exactly as he said ;—
The spark arrived, and then approached the bed

('Twas near the foot), then 'tween the sheets he slid,
But God knows how he lay or what he did.
Astolphus and Joconde ne'er smelt a rat,
Nor ever dreamt of what their girl was at.
At length, when each had turned and oped his eyes,
Continual movement filled him with surprise.
The monarch softly said, "Why, how is this?
My friend has caten something, for in bliss
He revels on, and truly much I fear
His health will show it may be bought too dear."

This very sentiment Joconde bethought;
But Clod a breathing moment having caught,
Resumed his fun, and that so oft would seek,
He gratified his wishes for a week;
Then, watching carefully, he found once more
Our noble heroes had begun to snore,
On which he slyly took himself away
The road he came, and ere 'twas break of day.
The girl soon followed, since she justly feared
Still more fatigues; so off she quickly steered.

At length, when both the nobles were awake,
Astolphus said, "My friend, you rest should take;
'Twere better till to-morrow keep in bed,
Since sleep, with such fatigues, of course has fled."
"You talk at random," cried the Roman youth;
"More rest I fancy *you* require, in truth;
You've led a pretty life throughout the night."
"I?" said the king. "Why, I was weary quite,
So long I waited; you no respite gave,
But wholly seemed our little nymph t' enslave.

At length, to try if I from rage could keep,
I turned my back once more and went to sleep.
If you had willingly the belle resigned,
I was, my friend, to take a turn inclined ;
That had sufficed for *me*, since I, like you,
Perpetual motion never can pursue."

"Your raillery," the Roman youth replied,
Quite disconcerted, "pray now lay aside,
And talk of something else ; you've fully shown
That I'm your vassal ; and since *you* are grown
So fond that you to keep the girl desire,
E'en wholly to yourself, why, I'll retire ;
Do with her what you please, and we shall see
How long this *furor* will with you agree."

"It may," replied the king, "for ever last,
If every night like this I'm doomed to fast."

"Sire," said Joconde, "no longer let us thus
In terms of playful raillery discuss ;
Since such your pleasure, send me from your view."
On this the youthful monarch angry grew,
And many words between the friends arose ;—
The presence of the nymph Astolphus chose ;
To her they said, "Between us judge, sweet fair ;"
And everything was stated then with care.

The girl with blushing cheeks before them kneeled,
And the mysterious tale at once revealed.
Our heroes laughed ; the treach'ry vile excused ;
And gave the ring, which much delight diffused ;

Together with a handsome sum of gold,
Which soon a husband in her train enrolled,
Who for a maid the pretty fair one took ;
And then our heroes wand'ring pranks forsook,
With laurels covered, which in future times
Will make them famous through the Western climes ;
More glorious since they only cost, we find,
Those sweet attentions pleasing to the mind.

So many conquests proud of having made,
And over full the book of—those who'd played ;
Said gay Astolphus, " We will now, my friend,
Return the shortest road, and *poaching* end ;
If false our mates, yet we'll console ourselves
That many others have inconstant elves.
Perhaps in things a change will be one day,
And only *tender* flames Love's torch display ;
But now it seems some evil star presides,
And Hymen's flock the devil surely rides.
Besides, vile fiends the universe pervade,
Whose constant aim is mortals to degrade,
And cheat us to our noses if they can
(Hell's imps in human shape, disgrace to man !)
Perhaps these wretches have bewitched our wives,
And made us fancy errors in their lives.
Then let us, like good citizens, our days
In future pass amidst domestic ways ;
Our absence may indeed restore their hearts,
For jealousy oft virtuous truths imparts."

In this Astolphus certainly believed ;
The friends returned, and kindly were received ;

A little scolding first assailed the ear,
But blissful kisses banished every fear.
To balls and banquets all themselves resigned ;
Of dwarf or valet nothing more we find ;
Each with his wife contentedly remained :—
'Tis thus alone true happiness is gained.

THE CUDGELLED AND CONTENTED
CUCKOLD

SOME time ago from Rome, in smart array,
  A younger brother homeward bent his way,
    Not much improved, as frequently 's the case
With those who travel to that famous place.
Upon the road oft finding, where he stayed,
Delightful wines and handsome belle or maid,
With careless ease he loitered up and down.
One day there passed him in a country town,
Attended by a page, a lady fair,
Whose charming form and all-engaging air,
At once his bosom fired with fond desire;
And nearer still her beauties to admire,
He most gallantly saw her safely home;—
Attentions charm the sex where'er we roam.

  Our thoughtless rambler pleasures always sought;
From Rome this spark had num'rous pardons brought;
But, as to virtues (this too oft we find),
He'd left them with his Holiness *—behind!

  The lady was by every one confessed
Of beauty, youth, and elegance possessed;

* The Pope.

She wanted nought to form her bliss below
But one whose love would ever fondly flow.

Indeed, so fickle proved this giddy youth
That nothing long would please his heart or tooth;
Howe'er, he earnestly inquired her name,
And every other circumstance the same.
"She's lady," they replied, "to great Squire Good,
Who's almost bald from age, 'tis understood;
But as he's rich, and high in rank appears,
Why, that's a recompense, you know, for years."

These facts our young gallant no sooner gained
But ardent hopes at once he entertained;
To wily plots his mind he quickly bent,
And to a neighb'ring town his servants sent;
Then, at the house where dwelled our noble squire
His humble services proposed for hire.

Pretending every sort of work he knew,
He soon a fav'rite with old Square-toes grew,
Who (first advising with his charming mate)
Chief falc'ner made him o'er his fine estate.

The new domestic much the lady pleased;
He watched, and eagerly the moment seized
His ardent passion boldly to declare,
In which he showed a novice had no share.

'Twas managed well, for nothing but the chase
Could Square-toes tempt to quit her fond embrace,
And then our falc'ner must his steps attend—
The very time he wished at home to spend.

The lady similar emotions showed ;
For opportunity their bosoms glowed ;
And who will feel in argument so bold,
When this I say, the contrary to hold ?
At length with pity Cupid saw the case,
And kindly lent his aid to their embrace.

One night the lady said, with eager eyes,
" My dear, among our servants, which d'ye prize
For moral conduct most and upright heart ? "
To this her spouse replied, " The faithful part
Is with the falc'ner found, I must decide :
To him my life I'd readily confide."

" Then you are wrong," said she ; " most truly so,
For he's a good-for-nothing wretch, I know ;
You'll scarcely credit it, but t'other day
He had the barefaced impudence to say
He loved me much, and then his passion pressed :
I'd nearly fallen, I was so distressed.
To tear his eyes out I designed at first,
And e'en to choke this wretch, of knaves the worst.
By prudence solely was I then restrained,
For fear the world should think his point was gained.
The better then to prove his dark intent,
I feigned an inclination to consent,
And in the garden promised, as to-night,
I'd near the pear-tree meet this roguish wight.
Said I, ' My husband never moves from hence ;
No jealous fancy, but to show the sense
He entertains of my pure, virtuous life,
And fond affection for a loving wife.

Thus circumstanced, your wishes, see, are vain,
Unless when he's asleep a march I gain,
And softly stealing from his torpid side,
With trembling steps I to my lover glide.'
So things remain, my dear;—an odd affair."
On this old Square-toes 'gan to curse and swear;
But his fond rib most earnestly besought
His rage to stifle, as she clearly thought
He might in person, if he'd take the pain,
Secure the rascal and redress obtain.
"You know," said she, "the tree is near the door,
Upon the left, and bears of fruit great store;
But if I may my sentiments express,
In cap and petticoats you'd best to dress;
His insolence is great, and you'll be right
To give your strokes with double force to-night;
Well work his back; flat lay him on the ground:—
A rascal! honourable ladies round
No doubt he many times has served the same;
'Tis such impostors characters defame."

To rouse his wrath the story quite sufficed;
The spouse resolved to do as she advised,
Howe'er, to dupe him was an easy lot.
The hour arrived; his dress he soon had got;
Away he ran with anxious, fond delight,
In hopes the wily spark to trap that night.
But no one there our easy fool could see,
And while he waited near the fav'rite tree,
Half dead with cold, the falc'ner slyly stole
To her who had so well contrived the whole;

Time, place, and disposition all combined—
The loving pair to mutual joys resigned.

When our expert gallant had with the dame
An hour or more indulged his ardent flame,
Though forced at length to quit the loving lass,
'Twas not without the fav'rite parting glass ;
He then the garden sought, where long the squire
Upon the knave had wished to vent his ire.

No sooner he the silly husband spied,
But, feigning 'twas the wily wife he eyed,
At once he cried, " Ah, vilest of the sex !
Are these thy tricks, so good a man to vex ?
Oh, shame upon thee ! thus to treat his love,
As pure as snow, descending from above.
I could not think thou hadst so base a heart,
But clear it is thou need'st a friendly part,
And that I'll act : I asked this rendezvous
With full intent to see if thou wert true ;
And, God be praised, without a loose design,
To plunge in luxuries pronounced divine.
Protect me, Heaven ! poor sinner that I'm here !
To guard thy honour I will persevere.
My worthy master could I thus disgrace ?
Thou wanton baggage with unblushing face,
Thee on the spot I'll instantly chastise,
And then thy husband of the fact advise."

The fierce harangue o'er Square-toes pleasure spread,
Who, mutt'ring 'tween his teeth, with fervour said :

"O gracious Lord ! to Thee my thanks are due—
To have a wife so chaste—a man so true ! "
But presently he felt upon his back
The falc'ner's cudgel vigorously thwack,
Who soundly basted him as on he ran,
To gain the house, with terror pale and wan.

The squire had wished his trusty man, no doubt,
Had not at cudgelling been quite so stout ;
But since he showed himself so true a friend,
And with his actions could such prudence blend,
The master fully pardoned what he knew,
And quickly to his wife in bed he flew,
When he related everything that passed.
" Were we," cried he, " a hundred years to last,
My lovely dear, we ne'er on earth should find
A man so faithful and so well inclined.
I'd have him take within our town a wife,
And you and I'll regard him during life."
" In that," replied the lady, " we agree,
And heartily thereto I pledged will be."

THE HUSBAND-CONFESSOR

WHEN Francis (named the First) o'er Frenchmen reigned,
  In Italy young Arthur laurels gained,
And oft such daring valour showed in fight,
With every honour he was made a knight;
The monarch placed the spur upon his heel,
That all around his proper worth might feel.
Then household deities at home he sought,
Where, not at prayers, his beauteous dame he caught.
He'd left her, truly, quite dissolved in tears;
But now the belle had bid adieu to fears,
And oft was dancing joyously around
With all the company that could be found.

  Gallants in crowds Sir Arthur soon perceived;
At sight of these the knight was sorely grieved;
And, turning in his mind how best to act,
Cried he, "Can this be truly held a fact,
That I've been worthy, while I'd fame in view,
Of cuckoldom at home, and knighthood too?
It ought to be but half:—the truth let's know;
From constancy the purest blessings flow."
Then like a father-confessor he dressed,
And took his seat where priests their flock confessed.

His lady absolution sought that day,
And on her knees before him 'gan to pray;
The minor sins were told with downcast eyes,
And then for hearing those of larger size
The husband-confessor prepared his ears.
Said she, "Good father" ('mid a flood of tears),
"My bed receives (the fault, I fear, 's not slight)
A gentleman, a parson, and a knight."
Still more had followed, but, by rage o'ercome,
Sir Arthur cut the thread, and she was mum;
Though, doubtless, had the fair been let proceed,
Quite long her litany had been decreed.

The husband, in a rage, exclaimed, "Thou jade!
A parson, say'st thou?   T' whom dost think thou'st made
This curst confession?"   "To my spouse," cried she.
"I saw you enter here, and came with glee,
Supposing you'd a trick to raise surprise.
Howe'er, 'tis strange that one so very wise
The riddle should not fully comprehend:—
A knight the king created you, my friend;
A gentleman your rank was long ago:
A parson you have made *yourself*, you know."

"Good heavens!" exclaimed the knight, "'tis very clear,
And I a blockhead surely must appear."

THE COBBLER

W E'RE told that once a cobbler, Blase by name,
A wife had got whose charms were high in fame;
But as it happened that their cash was spent,
The honest couple to a neighbour went,
A corn-factor by trade, not over wise,
To whom they stated facts without disguise,
And begged, with falt'ring voice denoting care,
That he of wheat would half a measure spare,
Upon their note, which readily he gave,
And all advantages desired to waive.

The time for payment come, the money used,
The cash our factor would not be refused ;
Of writs he talked, attorneys, and distress;
The reason—Heaven can tell, and you may guess ;
In short, 'twas clear our gay gallant desired
To cheer the wife, whose beauty all admired.

Said he, "What anxiously I wish to get
You've plenty stored, and never wanted yet.
You surely know my meaning ? " " Yes," she cried ;
" I'll turn it in my mind, and we'll decide
How best to act."   Away she quickly flew,
And Blase informed what Ninny had in view.

"Zounds!" said the cobbler, "we must see, my dear,
To hook this little sum :—the way is clear ;
No risk, I'm confident ; so prithee run
And tell him I've a journey just begun,
That he may hither come and have his will ;
But ere he touch thy lips demand the bill ;
He'll not refuse the boon, I'm very sure.
Meantime myself I'll hide, and all secure,
The note obtained, cough loudly, strong, and clear ;
Twice let it be, that I may plainly hear ;
Then forth I'll sally from my lurking-place,
And, spite of folly's frowns, prevent disgrace."

The plot succeeded as the pair desired ;
The cobbler laughed, and all his scheme admired.

A purse-proud cit. thereon observed and swore,
"'Twere better to have coughed when all was o'er ;
Then you, all three, would have enjoyed your wish,
And been in future all as mute as fish."

"Oh, sir!" replied the cobbler's wife, at ease,
"Do you suppose that *we* can hope to please,
And like your ladies full of sense appear ? "
(For two were seated with his wedded dear.)
"Perhaps *my lady* 'd act as you describe,
But every one such prudence don't imbibe."

THE PEASANT AND HIS ANGRY
LORD

ONCE on a time, as hist'ry's page relates,
A lord, possessed of many large estates,
Was angry with a poor and humble clod,
Who tilled his grounds and feared his very nod.
Th' offence (as often happens) was but small,
But on him, vowed the peer, his rage should fall.
Said he, " A halter, rascal, you deserve;
You'll never from the gallows-turnpike swerve :
Or soon or late you swinging will be found :
Who, born for hanging, ever yet was drowned ?
Howe'er, you'll smile to hear my lenient voice;
Observe, three punishments await your choice ;
Take which you will.   The first is, you shall eat
Of strongest garlic thirty heads complete ;
No drink you'll have between, nor sleep, nor rest;
You know a breach of promise I detest.
Or on your shoulders further I propose
To give you, with a cudgel, thirty blows.
Or, if more pleasing, that you truly pay
The sum of thirty pounds without delay."

The peasant 'gan to turn things in his mind :—
Said he, "To take the heads I'm not inclined,

No drink, you say, between :—that makes it worse ;
To eat the garlic thus would prove a curse.
Nor can I suffer on my tender back
That, with a cudgel, thirty blows you thwack."
Still harder thirty pounds to pay appeared ;
Uncertain how to act, he hanging feared.
The noble peer he begged, upon his knees,
His penitence to hear and sentence ease.
But mercy dwelled not with the angry lord ;—
" Is this," cried he, " the answer ?   Bring a cord."
The peasant, trembling lest his life was sought,
The garlic chose, which presently was brought.

    Upon a dish my lord the number told ;
Clod no way liked the garlic to behold.
With piteous mien the garlic-head he took,
Then on it num'rous ways was led to look,
And grumbling much, began to spit and eat,
Just like a cat with mustard on her meat ;
To touch it with his tongue he durst not do ;
He knew not how to act or what pursue.
The peer, delighted at the man's distress,
The garlic made him bite, and chew, and press,
Then gulp it down as if delicious fare.
The first he passed ; the second made him swear ;
The third he found was every whit as sad,
He wished the devil had it, 'twas so bad.
In short, when at the twelfth our wight arrived,
He thought his mouth and throat of skin deprived ;
Said he, " Some drink I earnestly entreat."
" What, Greg'ry," cried my lord, " dost feel a heat ?

In thy repasts dost love to wet thy jaws ?
Well, well ! I won't object ; thou know'st my laws.
Much good may 't do thee.   Here, some wine, some wine !
Yet recollect, to drink since you design,
That afterward, my friend, you'll have to choose
The thirty blows, or thirty pounds to lose."
"But," cried the peasant, "I sincerely pray
Your lordship's goodness that the garlic may
Be taken in the account, for as to pelf,
Where can an humble lab'rer, like myself,
Expect the sum of thirty pounds to seize ? "
"Then," said the peer, "be cudgelled if you please ;
Take thirty thwacks ; for nought the garlic goes."
To moisten well his throat and ease his woes,
The peasant drank a copious draught of wine,
And then to bear the cudgel would resign.

A single blow he patiently endured ;
The second, howsoe'er, his patience cured ;
The third was more severe, and each was worse ;
The punishment he now began to curse.
Two lusty wights with cudgels thrashed his back,
And regularly gave him thwack and thwack ;
He cried, he roared, for grace he begged his lord,
Who marked each blow, and would no ease accord ;
But carefully observed, from time to time,
That lenity he always thought sublime ;
His gravity preserved ; considered too
The blows received and what continued due.

At length, when Greg'ry twenty strokes had got,
He piteously exclaimed, "If more's my lot

I never shall survive! Oh! pray forgive,
If you desire, my lord, that I should live."
"Then down with thirty pounds," replied the peer,
" Since you the blows so much pretend to fear.
I'm sorry for you ; but, if all the gold
Be not prepared, your godfather, I'm told,
Can lend a part ; yet, since so far you've been,
To flinch the rest you surely won't be seen. "

The wretched peasant to his lordship flew,
And trembling cried, " 'Tis up! the number view!"
A scrutiny was made, which nothing gained ;
No choice but pay the money now remained ;
This grieved him much, and o'er the fellow's face
The dewy drops were seen to flow apace.
All useless proved ;—the full demand he sent,
With which the peer expressed himself content.
Unlucky he whoe'er his lord offends !
To golden ore, howe'er, the proud man bends.

'Twas vain that Gregory a pardon prayed ;
For trivial faults the peasant dearly paid ;—
His throat inflamed—his tender back well beat—
His money gone—and all to make complete,
Without the least deduction for the pain
The blows and garlic gave the trembling swain.

THE MULETEER

THE Lombard princes oft pervade my mind ;
   The present tale Boccacc relates, you'll find ;
   Agiluf was the noble monarch's name ;
Teudelingua he married, beauteous dame,
The last king's widow, who had left no heir,
And whose dominions proved our prince's share.

No beauty round compare could with the queen,
And every blessing on the throne was seen,
When Cupid, in a playful moment, came,
And o'er Agiluf's stable placed his flame ;
There left it carelessly to burn at will,
Which soon began a muleteer to fill
With love's all-powerful, all-consuming fire,
That nought controls, and youthful breasts desire.

The muleteer was pleasing to the sight,
Gallant, good-humoured, airy, and polite,
And every way his humble birth belied ;·
A handsome person, nor was sense denied ;
He showed it well, for when the youth beheld,
With eyes of love, the queen, who all excelled,
And every effort anxiously had made
To stop the flames that would his heart invade,

When vain it proved, he took a prudent part :—
Who can, like Cupid, manage wily art ?
Whate'er stupidity we may discern,
Ilis pupils more within a day can learn
Than masters knowledge in the schools can gain,
Though they in study should ten years remain ;
The lowest clown he presently inspires
With every tendency that love requires ;
Of this our present tale's a proof direct,
And none that feel, its truths will e'er suspect.

The am'rous muleteer his thoughts employed,
Consid'ring how his wish might be enjoyed.
Without success to certainty were brought,
Life seemed to him not worth a slender thought ;
To hazard everything ;—to live or die !
Possession have !—or in the grave to lie !

The Lombard custom was, that when the king,
Who slept not with his queen (a common thing
In other countries too), desired to greet
His royal consort, and in bed to meet,
A night-gown solely o'er his back he threw,
And then proceeded to the interview,
Knocked softly at the door, on which a fair,
Who waited on the queen with anxious care,
Allowed the prince to enter ;—took his light
(Which only glimmered in the midst of night),
Then put it out, and quickly left the room :—
A little lantern to dispel the gloom,
With waxen taper that emitted rays—
In diff'rent countries various are their ways !

Our wily, prying, crafty muleteer
Knew well these forms were current through the year.
He, like the king, at night himself equipped,
And to the queen's superb apartment slipped.

His face concealed the fellow tried to keep;
The waiting dame was more than half asleep.
The lover got access.   Soon all was clear;
The prince's coming he had but to fear;
And, as the latter had, throughout the day,
The chase attended an extensive way,
'Twas more than probable he'd not be led
(Since such fatigue he'd had) to quit his bed.

Perfumed, quite neat, and lively as a bird,
Our spark (safe entered) uttered not a word.
'Twas often customary with the king,
When state affairs, or other weighty thing,
Displeasure gave, to take of love his fill,
Yet let his tongue the while continue still,—
A singularity we needs must own;
With this the wife was long familiar grown.

Our am'rous wight more joys than one received,
If our narrator of the tale's believed
(In bed a muleteer is worth three kings,
And value oft is found in humble things).
The queen began to think her husband's rage
Had proved a stimulus such wars to wage,
And made him wondrous stout in pleasure's sport,
Though all the while his thoughts were—'bout the court.

With perfect justice Heaven its gift bestows ;
But equal talents all should not compose.
The prince's virtues doubtless were designed
To take command and govern o'er mankind.
The lawyer points of difficulty views,
Decides with judgment, and the truth pursues.
In Cupid's scenes the muleteer succeeds—
Each has his part—none universal meeds.

With pleasures feasted, our gallant retired
Before the morn fresh blushes had acquired.
But scarcely had he left the tender scene
Ere King Agiluf came to see his queen,
Who much surprise expressed, and to him said,
" My dear, I know your love, but from this bed
You'll recollect how recently you went,
And having wonders done, should be content.
For Heaven's sake, consider more your health ;
'Tis dearer far to me than Crœsus' wealth."

Within the royal breast suspicions rose,
But nothing then the monarch would disclose.
He instantly withdrew without a word—
His sentiments to speak had been absurd—
And to the stable flew, since he believed
The circumstances which his bosom grieved,
Whate'er mysterious doubts might then appear,
Proceeded from some am'rous muleteer.

When round the dorture he began to creep,
The troop appeared as if dissolved in sleep;

And so they truly were, save our gallant,
Whose terrors made him tremble, sigh, and pant.
No light the king had got; it still was dark;
Agiluf groped about to find the spark,
Persuaded that the culprit might be known
By rapid beating of the pulse alone.
The thought was good; to feel the prince began,
And at the second venture found his man,
Who, whether from the pleasures he'd enjoyed,
Or fear, or dread discov'ry to avoid,
Experienced (spite of every wily art)
At once quick beating of the pulse and heart.
In doubt how this adventure yet might end,
He thought to seem asleep would him befriend.

Meanwhile the king, though not without much pains,
Obtained the scissors used for horses' manes.
"With these," said he, "I'll mark the fond gallant,
That I may know again the one I want."

The monarch from the muleteer with care,
In front snipped off a bulky lock of hair.
This having done, he suddenly withdrew;
But carelessly away the trophy threw;
Of which the sly gallant advantage took,
And thus the prince's subtle project shook;
For instantly began our artful spark
His fellow-servants like himself to mark.

When day arrived the monarch was surprised
To see each muleteer alike disguised;

No hair in front of either now was seen.
"Why, how is this?" said he.   "What can it mean?
Fifteen or more, if I believe my sight,
My wife has satisfied this very night.
Well! well! he'll now escape if mum he prove,
But there again, I trust, he ne'er shall move."

THE SERVANT-GIRL JUSTIFIED

BOCCACE alone is not my only source;
T' another shop I now shall have recourse;
    Though, certainly, this famed Italian wit
Has many stories for my purpose fit.
But since of diff'rent dishes we should taste,
Upon an ancient work my hands I've placed,
Where full a hundred narratives are told,
And various characters we may behold.
From life, Navarre's fair queen the fact relates;
My story int'rest in her page creates;
Beyond dispute from her we always find
Simplicity with striking art combined.
Yet, whether 'tis the queen who writes or not,
I shall, as usual, here and there allot
Whate'er additions requisite appear—
Without such licence I'd not persevere,
But quit, at once, narrations of the sort;
Some may be long, though others are too short.

    Let us proceed, howe'er (our plan explained);
A pretty servant-girl a man retained.
She pleased his eye, and presently he thought
With ease she might to am'rous sports be brought;

He proved not wrong; the wench was blithe and gay,
A buxom lass, most able every way.

At dawn, one summer's morn, the spark was led
To rise, and leave his wife asleep in bed;
He sought at once the garden, where he found
The servant-girl collecting flowers around
To make a nosegay for his better half,
Whose birthday 'twas :—he soon began to laugh,
And while the ranging of the flowers he praised,
The servant's neckerchief he slyly raised.
Who suddenly, on feeling of the hand,
Resistance feigned, and seemed to make a stand;
But since these liberties were nothing new,
They other fun and frolics would pursue;
The nosegay at the fond gallant was thrown;
The flowers he kissed, and now more ardent grown,
They romped and rattled, played and skipped around.
At length the fair one fell upon the ground;
Our am'rous spark advantage took of this,
And nothing with the couple seemed amiss.

Unluckily, a neighbour's prying eyes
Beheld their playful pranks with great surprise;
She, from her window, could the scene o'erlook.
When this the fond gallant observed, he shook;
Said he, "By heavens! our frolicking is seen
By that old haggard, envious, prying quean;
But do not heed it."   Instantly he chose
To run and wake his wife, who quickly rose;—
So much the dame he fondled and caressed,
The garden-walk she took at his request,

To have a nosegay, where he played anew
Pranks just the same as those of recent view,
Which highly gratified our lady fair,
Who felt disposed and would at eve repair
To her good neighbour, whom she bursting found
With what she'd seen that morn upon the ground.

The usual greetings o'er, our envious dame,
With scowling brow, exclaimed, " My dear, your fame
I love too much not fully to detail
What I have witnessed, and with truth bewail.
Will you continue in your house to keep
A girl whose conduct almost makes me weep ?
Anon I'd kick her from your house, I say ;
The strumpet should not stay another day."
The wife replied, " You surely are deceived ;
An honest, virtuous creature she's believed."
" Well, I can easily, my friend, suppose,"
Rejoined the neighbour, " whence this favour flows ;
But look about, and be convinced.   This morn,
From my own window (true as you are born),
Within the garden I your husband spied,
And presently the servant-girl I eyed ;
At one another various flowers they threw,
And then the minx a little graver grew."
" I understand you," cried the list'ning fair ;
" You are deceived—myself alone was there."

NEIGHBOUR

But patience, if you please : attend, I pray :
You've no conception what I meant to say.

The playful fair was actively employed
In plucking am'rous flowers :—they kissed and toyed.

WIFE

'Twas clearly I, howe'er, for *her* you took.

NEIGHBOUR

The flowers for bosoms quickly they forsook ;
Large handfuls frequently they seemed to grasp,
And every beauty in its turn to clasp.

WIFE

But still, why think you, friend, it was not I ?
Has not your spouse with *you* a right to try
What freaks he likes ?

NEIGHBOUR

   But then, upon the ground
This girl was thrown, and never cried nor frowned ;
You laugh.

WIFE

  Indeed I do, since 'twas myself.

NEIGHBOUR

A flannel petticoat displayed the elf.

WIFE

'Twas mine.

NEIGHBOUR

  Be patient, and inform me, pray,
If this were worn by you or her to-day.

There lies the point, for, if you'll me believe,
Your husband did—the most you can conceive.

WIFE

How hard of credence! —'twas myself, I vow.

NEIGHBOUR

Oh! that's conclusive; I'll be silent now;
Though truly I am led to think my eyes
Are pretty sharp, and much I feel surprise
At what you say;—in fact, I would have sworn
I saw them thus at romps this very morn;
Excuse the hint, and do not turn her off.

WIFE

Why, turn her off?—the very thought I scoff;
She serves me well.

NEIGHBOUR

      And so, it seems, is taught;
By all means keep her then, since thus she's thought.

THE THREE GOSSIPS' WAGER

A S o'er their wine one day three gossips sat,
   Discoursing various pranks in pleasant chat,
   Each had a loving friend, and two of these
Most clearly managed matters at their ease.

  Said one, " A princely husband I have got,
A better in the world there's surely not ;
With *him* I can adjust as humour fits,
No need to rise at early dawn, like cits,
To prove to him that two and three make *four*,
Or ask his leave to ope or shut the door."

  " Upon my word," replied another fair,
" If he were mine, I openly declare,
To judge from what so pleasantly you say,
I'd make a present of him New Year's Day ;
For pleasure never gives me full delight
Unless a little pain the bliss invite.
No doubt your husband moves as he is led ;
Thank Heaven a diff'rent mortal claims my bed ;
To take him in great nicety we need ;
But, howsoe'er, at times I can succeed ;
The satisfaction doubly then is felt ;
In fond emotion bosoms freely melt.

With neither of you, husband or gallant
Would I exchange, though these so much you vaunt."

On this the third with candour interfered ;
She thought that oft the God of Love appeared
Good husbands playfully to fret and vex,
Sometimes to rally couples, then perplex ;
But warmer as the conversation grew,
She, anxious that each disputant might view
Herself victorious (or believe it so),
Exclaimed, " If either of you wish to show
Who's in the right, with argument have done,
And let us practise some new scheme of fun
To dupe our husbands ; she who don't succeed
Shall pay a forfeit."   All replied, " Agreed."
" But then," continued she, " we ought to take
An oath that we will full discov'ry make
To one another of the various facts,
Without disguising even trifling acts ;
And then good upright Macæ shall decide."
Thus things arranged, the ladies homeward plied.

She 'mong the three who felt the most constraint,
Adored a youth, contemporaries paint
Well-made and handsome, but with beardless chin,
Which led the pair a project to begin ;
For yet no opportunity they'd found
T' enjoy their wishes save by stealth around ;
Most ardently they sought to be at ease,
And 'twas agreed the lucky thought to seize,
That like a chambermaid he should be dressed,
And then proceed to execute the jest,

Attend upon the wily, wedded pair,
And offer services with modest air
And downcast eyes.   The husband on her leered,
And in her favour prepossessed appeared,
In hopes one day to find those pleasing charms
Resigned in secret to his longing arms.
Such pretty cheeks and sparkling eyes, he thought,
Had ne'er till then his roving fancy caught.
The girl was hired, but seemingly with pain,
Since prudence ultimately might complain
That (maid and master both so very young)
'Twould not be wonderful if things went wrong.

At first the husband inattention showed,
And scarcely on the maid a look bestowed ;
But presently he changed his conduct quite,
And presents gave, with promises not slight.
At length the servant feigned to lend an ear,
And anxious seemed obliging to appear.

The trap our cunning lovers having laid,
One eve this message brought the smiling maid :—
" My lady, sir, is ill, and rest requires ;
To sleep alone to-night she much desires."

To grant the master's wish the girl was led,
And they together hurried off to bed.

The husband 'tween the sheets himself had placed ;
The nymph was in her petticoat, unlaced ;
When suddenly appeared the wily wife,
And promised harmony was turned to strife.

"Are these your freaks?" cried she, with marked
    surprise.
"Your usual dish, it seems, then don't suffice;
You want, indeed, to have some nicer fare?
A little sooner, by the saints I swear,
You'd me a pretty trick, 'tis clear, have shown,
And doubtless, then, tit-bits to keep been prone.
This, howsoe'er, to get you're not designed,
So elsewhere you may try what you can find.
And as to you, Miss Prettyface, you jade—
Good heavens! to think a paltry servant-maid
Should rival me! I'll beat you black and blue!
The bread I eat, indeed, must be for you?
But I know better, and indeed am clear
Not one around will fancy I appear
So void of charms, so faded, withered, lost,
That I should out of doors at once be tossed.
But I will manage matters—I design
This girl no other bed shall have than mine;
Then who so bold to touch her there will dare?
Come, Miss, let's to my room at once repair;
Away—your things to-morrow you can seek.
If scandal 'twould not spread around, I'd wreak
My vengeance instantly, and turn you out;
But I am lenient, and desire no rout.
Perhaps your ruin may be saved by care,
So night and day your company I'll share;
No more my bosom then will feel dismay,
For I shall see that you no frolics play."

On this the trembling girl, o'ercome with fears,
Held down her head and seemed to hide her tears;

Picked up her clothes and quickly stole away,
As if afraid her mistress more might say;
And hoped to act the maid while Sol gave light,
But play at ease the fond gallant at night.
At once she filled two places in the house,
And thought in both the husband she should chouse,
Who blessed his stars that he'd escaped so well,
And sneaked alone to rest within his cell;
While our gay, am'rous pair advantage took
To play at will and every solace hook,
Convinced most thoroughly, once lovers kissed,
That opportunity should ne'er be missed.
Here ends the trick our wily gossip played;
But now let's see the plot another laid.

The second dame, whose husband was so meek
That only from her lips the truth he'd seek,
When seated with him 'neath a pear-tree's shade,
Contrived at ease and her arrangement made.
The story I shall presently relate :—
The butler, strong, well dressed, and full of prate,
Who often made the other servants trot,
Stood near when madam hit upon her plot,
To whom she said, "I wish the fruit to taste;"
On which the man prepared with every haste
To climb the tree, and off the produce shook;
But while above, the fellow gave a look
Upon the ground below, and feigned he saw
The spouse and wife—do more than kiss and paw.
The servant rubbed his eyes, as if in doubt,
And cried: "Why, truly, sir, if you're so stout
That you must revel 'mid your lady's charms,

Pray elsewhere take her to your longing arms,
Where you at ease may frolic hours or days,
Without my witnessing your loving ways.
Indeed, I'm quite surprised at what I spy:
In public, 'neath a tree such pranks to try !
And, if you don't a servant's presence heed,
With decency, howe'er, you should proceed.
What ! still go on ?   For shame, I say, for shame !
Pray wait till by-and-by ; you're much to blame.
Besides, the nights are long enough, you'll find ;
Heaven genial joys for privacy designed.
And why this place, when you've nice chambers got ? "
" What," cried the lady, " says this noisy sot ?
He surely dreams.   Where can he learn these tales ?
Come down ; let's see what 'tis the fellow ails."
Down William came.   " How ? " said the master, " how ? "
Are we at play ? "

WILLIAM

Not now, sir ; no, not now.

HUSBAND

Why, when then, friend ?

WILLIAM

While I was in the tree,
Alive, sir, flay me, if I did not see
You on the verdant lawn my lady lay,
And kiss, and toy, and other frolics play.

WIFE

'Twere surely better if thou held'st thy tongue,
Or thou'lt a beating get before 'tis long.

HUSBAND

No, no, my dear, he's mad; and I design
The fellow in a madhouse to confine.

WILLIAM

Is't folly, pray, to see what we behold ?

WIFE

What *hast* thou seen ?

WILLIAM

                    What I've already told :—
My master and yourself at Cupid's game,
Or else the tree's enchanted, I proclaim.

WIFE

Enchanted!   Nonsense.   Such a sight to see !

HUSBAND

To know the truth myself, I'll climb the tree,
Then you the fact will quickly from me learn ;
We may believe what we ourselves discern.

Soon as the master they above descried,
And that below our pair he sharply eyed,
The butler took the lady in his arms,
And grew at once familiar with her charms.
At sight of this the husband gave a yell,
Made haste to reach the ground, and nearly fell ;
Such liberties he wished at once to stop,
Since what he'd seen had nearly made him drop.

"How! how!" cried he; "what! e'en before my sight?"
"What *can* you mean?" said she without affright.

HUSBAND

Dar'st thou to ask again?

WIFE

And why not, pray?

HUSBAND

Fine, pretty doings!   Presently you'll say
That what I've seen 'tis folly to believe.

WIFE

Too much is this; such accusations grieve.

HUSBAND

Thou didst most cheer'ly suffer his embrace.

WIFE

I?   Why, you dream!

HUSBAND

This seems a curious case.
My reason's flown! or have I lost my eyes?

WIFE

Can you suppose my character I prize
So very little that these pranks I'd play
Before your face, when I might every day
Find minutes to divert myself at will,
And (if I liked such frolics) take my fill?

HUSBAND

I know not what to think nor what to do;
P'r'aps this same tree can tricks at will pursue;
Let's see again."   Aloft he went once more,
And William acted as he'd done before;
But now the husband saw the playful squeeze
Without emotion, and returned at ease.
"To find the cause," said he, "no longer try;
The tree's enchanted, we may well rely."

  "Since that's the fact," replied the cunning jade,
"To burn it, quickly, William, seek for aid;
The tree accurst no longer shall remain."
Her will the servant wished not to restrain,
But soon some workmen brought, who felled the tree,
And wondered what the fault our fair could see.
"Down hew it," cried the lady, "that's your task;
More concerns you not; folly 'tis to ask."

  Our second gossip thus obtained success;
But now the third: we'll see if she had less.

  To female friends she often visits paid,
And various pastimes there had daily played;
A leering lover who was weary grown
Desired one night she'd meet him quite alone.
"Two, if you will," replied the smiling fair;
"A trifle 'tis you ask, and I'll repair
Where'er you wish, and we'll recline at ease;
My husband I can manage, if I please,
While thus engaged."   The parties soon agreed;
But still the lady for her wits had need,

Since her dear man from home but rarely went,
No pardons sought at Rome, but was content
With what he nearer got, while his sweet wife
More fondness marked for gratifying life,
And ever anxious warmest zeal to show,
Was always wishing distant scenes to know.
As pilgrim oft she'd trod a foreign road,
But now desired those ancient ways t' explode;
A plan more rare and difficult she sought,
And round her toe our wily dame bethought
To tie a pack-thread, fastened to the door,
Which opened to the street; then feigned to snore
Beside her husband, Harry Berlinguier
(So, usually, they named her wedded dear).

Howe'er, so cunningly with him she dealt
That Harry turned, and soon the pack-thread felt,
Which raised distrust, and led him to suspect
Some bad design the thread was meant t' effect.

A little time, as if asleep, he lay,
Considering how to act or what to say;
Then rose (his spouse believing not awake),
And softly treading, lest the room should shake,
The pack-thread followed to the outer door,
And thence concluded (what he might deplore)
That his dear partner from her faith would stray,
And some gallant that night designed to play
The lover's part and draw the secret clue,
When she would rise, and with him freaks pursue,
While he (good husband!) quietly in bed
Might sleep, not dreaming that his wife had fled.

For otherwise, what use such pains to take ?
A visit cuckoldom, perhaps, might make ;
An honour that he'd willingly decline ;
On which he studied how to countermine,
And like a sentinel moved to and fro,
To watch if any one should thither go
To pull the string, that he could see with ease,
And then he'd instantly the culprit seize.

The reader will perceive, we may suppose,
Besides the entrance which the husband chose,
On t' other side a door, where our gallant
Could enter readily, as he might want,
And there the spark a chambermaid let in ;—
Oft servants prone are found a bribe to win.

While Berlinguier thus watched around and round,
The friends with one another pleasures found ;
But Heaven alone knows how or what they were—
No fact transpired save all was free from care ;
So well the servant kept the careful watch
That not a chance was given the pair to catch.

The spark at dawn the lady left alone,
And ere the husband came the bird was flown ;
Then Harry, weary, took his place again,
Complaining that he'd felt such racking pain,
And dreading lest alarms her breast should seize,
Within another room he'd sought for ease.

Two days had passed, when madam thought once more
To set the thread, as she had done before ;

Then, soon as Berlinguier perceived the trick,
He left the bed, pretending he was sick,
Resumed his post ; again the lover came,
And with my lady played the former game.

The scheme so well succeeded that the pair
Thrice wished to try the wily pack-thread snare ;
The husband with the colic moved away,
His place the bold gallant resumed till day.

At length their ardour 'gan, it seems, to cool,
And Harry they no longer tried to fool ;
'Twas time to seek the myst'ry of the plot,
Since to three acts the comedy was got.

At midnight, when the spark had left the bed,
A servant, by his orders, drew the thread ;
On whom the husband, without fear, laid hold,
And with him entered like a soldier bold,
Not then supposing he'd a valet seized.
Well timed it proved, howe'er ;—the lady pleased
Her voice to raise on hearing what was said,
And through the house confusion quickly spread.

The valet now before them bent the knee,
And openly declared he came to see
The chambermaid, whom he was wont to greet,
And by the thread to rouse when time to meet.

" Are these your knavish tricks ? " replied the dame,
With eyes upon her maid that darted flame.

"When I by chance observed about your toe
A thread one night, I then resolved to know
Your scheme in full, and round my own I tied
A clue, on which I thoroughly relied,
To catch this gay gallant, that you pretend
Your husband will become, I apprehend.
Be that as 'twill, to-night from hence you go."
"My dear," said Berlinguier, "I'd fain say no;
Let things remain until to-morrow, pray;"
And then my lady presently gave way.
A fortune Harry on the girl bestowed;
The like our valet to his master owed;
To church the happy couple smiling went—
They'd known each other long, and were content.

   Thus ended, then, the third and last amour;
The trio hastened Macæ to implore
To say which gained the bet, who soon replied—
"I find it, friends, not easy to decide."

   The case hangs up, and there will long remain;
'Tis often thus when justice we'd obtain.

THE OLD MAN'S CALENDAR

OFT have I seen in wedlock, with surprise,
   That most forgot from which true bliss would rise ;
   When marriage for a daughter is designed,
The parents solely riches seem to mind ;
All other boons are left to Heaven above,
And sweet sixteen must sixty learn to love !
Yet still in other things they nicer seem,
Their chariot-horses and their oxen-team
Are truly matched ;—in height exact are *these*,
While *those* each shade alike must have to please ;
Without the choice 'twere wonderful to find,
Or coach or waggon travel for their mind.
The marriage journey full of cares appears
When couples match in neither souls nor years !
An instance of the kind I'll now detail :
The feeling bosom will such lots bewail !

   Quinzica (Richard), as the story goes,
Indulged his wife at balls and feasts and shows,
Expecting other duties she'd forget,
In which, howe'er, he disappointment met.
A judge in Pisa, Richard was, it seems,
In law most learned, wily in his schemes ;

But silver beard and locks too clearly told
He ought to have a wife of diff'rent mould;
Though he had taken one of noble birth,
Quite young, most beautiful, and formed for mirth—
(Bartholomea Galandi her name,
The lady's parents were of rank and fame)—
Our judge herein had little wisdom shown,
And sneering friends around were often known
To say his children ne'er could fathers lack;
At giving counsel some have got a knack,
Who, were they but at home to turn their eyes,
Might find, perhaps, they're not so over wise.

Quinzica then, perceiving that his powers
Fell short of what a bird like his devours,
T'excuse himself and satisfy his dear,
Pretended that no day within the year
To Hymen, as a saint, was e'er assigned,
In calendar or book of any kind,
When full attention to the god was paid:—
To aged sires a nice convenient aid;
But this the sex by no means fancy right.
Few days to pleasure could his heart invite;
At times the week entire he'd have a fast;
At others, say the day 'mong saints' was classed,
Though no one ever heard its holy name;—
Fast every Friday—Saturday the same,
Since Sunday followed, consecrated day.
Then Monday came;—still he'd abstain from play;
Each morning find excuse, but solemn feasts
Were days most sacred held by all the priests.

On abstinence, then, Richard lectures read,
And long before the time was always led,
By sense of right, from dainties to refrain ;
A period afterward would also gain ;
The like observed before and after Lent ;
And every feast had got the same extent.
These times were gracious for our aged man,
And never pass them was his constant plan.

Of patron saints he always had a list ;
Th' evangelists, apostles, none he missed ;
And that his scruples might have constant food,
Some days malign, he said, were understood ;
Then foggy weather ;—dog-days' fervent heat :
To seek excuses he was most complete,
And ne'er ashamed, but managed things so well,
Four times a year, by special grace, they tell,
Our sage regaled his youthful, blooming wife
A little with the sweets of marriage life.

With this exception he was truly kind,
Fine dresses, jewels, all to please her mind ;
But these are baubles which alone control
Those belles, like dolls, mere bodies void of soul.
Bartholomea was of diff'rent clay ;
Her only pleasure (as our hist'ries say)
To go in summer to the neighb'ring coast,
Where her good spouse a charming house could boast,
In which they took their lodging once a week.
At times they pleasure on the waves would seek,
As fishing with the lady would agree,
And she was wondrous partial to the sea ;

Though far to sail they always would refuse.
One day it happened, better to amuse,
Our couple diff'rent fishing-vessels took,
And skimmed the wave to try who most could hook
Of fish and pleasure ; and they laid a bet
The greatest number which of them should get.
On board they had a man or two at most,
And each the best adventure hoped to boast.

A certain pirate soon observed the ship
In which this charming lady made the trip,
And presently attacked and seized the same ;
But Richard's bark to shore in safety came ;
So near the land, or else he would not brave,
To any great extent, the stormy wave,
Or that the robber thought, if both he took,
He could not decently for favours look,
And he preferred those joys the fair bestow
To all the riches which to mortals flow.

Although a pirate, he had always shown
Much honour in his acts, as well was known ;
But Cupid's frolics were his heart's delight.
None truly brave can ever beauty slight ;
A sailor's always bold and kind and free,
Good lib'ral fellows, such they'll ever be ;
'Mong saints indeed 'twere vain their names to seek !
The man was good, howe'er, of whom we speak ;
His usual name was Pagamin Montegue.
For hours the lady's screams were heard a league,
While he each minute anxiously would seize
To cheer her spirits and her heart to please ;

T' attain his wish he every art combined ;
At length the lovely captive all resigned.

'Twas Cupid conquered, Cupid with his dart,
A thousand times more pirate in his art
Than Pagamin ; on bleeding hearts he preys,
But little quarter gives, nor grace displays.

To pay her ransom she'd enough of gold ;
For this her spouse was truly never cold ;
No fast nor festival therein appeared,
And her captivity he greatly feared.

This calendar o'erspread with rubric days
She soon forgot, and learned the pirate's ways ;
The matrimonial zone aside was thrown,
And only mentioned where the fact was known.

Our lawyer would his fingers sooner burn
Than have his wife but virtuous home return ;
By means of gold he entertained no doubt,
Her restoration might be brought about.
A passport from the pirate he obtained,
Then waited on him and his wish explained ;
To pay he offered whatsoe'er he'd ask ;
His terms accept, though hard perhaps the task.

The robber answered, " If my name around
Be not for honourable acts renowned,
'Tis quite unjust.   Your partner I'll restore
In health, without a ransom :—would you more ?
A friendship so respected, Heaven forefend !
Should ever, by my conduct, have an end.

The fair, whom you so ardently admire,
Shall to your arms return, as you desire.
Such pleasure to a friend I would not sell;
Convince me that she's yours and all is well;
For if another I to you should give
(And many that I've taken with me live),
I surely should incur a heavy blame.
I lately captured one, a charming dame
With auburn locks, a little fat, tall, young;
If she declare she does to you belong,
When you she's seen, I will the belle concede;
You'll take her instantly; I'll not impede."

The sage replied, "Your conduct's truly wise;
Such wondrous kindness fills me with surprise;
But since 'tis said that every trade must live,
The sum just mention;—I'll the ransom give.
No compliment I wish; my purse behold;—
You know the money presently is told.
Consider me a stranger now, I pray;
With you I'd equal probity display,
And so will act, I swear, as you shall see;
There's not a doubt the fair will go with me.
My word for this I would not have you take;—
You'll see how happy 'twill the lady make
To find me here; to my embrace she'll fly;
My only fear's that she of joy will die."

To them the charmer now was instant brought,
Who eyed her husband as beneath a thought;
Received him coldly, just as if he'd been
A stranger from Peru she ne'er had seen.

"Look," said Quinzica, "she's ashamed, 'tis plain;
So many lookers-on her love restrain:
But be assured, if we were left alone,
Around my neck her arms would soon be thrown."

"If this," replied the pirate, "you believe,
Attend her toilet; nought can then deceive."
Away they went, and closely shut the door;
When Richard said, "Thou darling of my store,
How canst thou thus behave?   My pretty dove,
'Tis thy Quinzica come to seek his love,
In all the same, except about his wife;
Dost in this face a change observe, my life?
'Tis grieving for thy loss that makes me ill;
Did ever I in aught deny thy will?
In dress or play could any thee exceed?
And hadst thou not whatever thou mightst need?
To please thee oft I made myself a slave;
Such thou art now; but thee again I crave.
Then what dost think about thy honour, dear?"
Said she, with ire, "I neither know nor fear.
Is this a time to guard it, do you say?
What pain was shown by any one, I pray,
When I was forced to wed a man like you,
Old, impotent, and hateful to the view,
While I was young and blooming as the morn,
Deserving, truly, something less forlorn,
And seemingly intended to possess
What Hymen best in store has got to bless?
For I was thought by all the world around
Most worthy every bliss in wedlock found.

Yet things took quite another turn with me:
In tune my husband never proved to be,
Except a feast or two throughout the year.
From Pagamin I met a diff'rent cheer.
Another lesson presently he taught;
The life's sweet pleasures more the pirate brought
In two short days than e'er I had from you
In those four years that only you I knew.

"Pray leave me, husband; let me have my will;
Insist not on my living with you still;
No calendars with Pagamin are seen—
Far better treated with the man I've been.
My other friends and you much worse deserved:
The spouse, for taking me when quite unnerved;
And they, for giving preference base to gold
To those pure joys—far better thought than told.
But Pagamin in every way can please;
And though no code he owns, yet all is ease.
Himself will tell you what has passed this morn;
His actions would a sov'reign prince adorn.
Such information may excite surprise,
But now the truth 'twere useless to disguise;
Nothing will gain belief, we've no one near
To witness our discourse:—adieu, my dear,
To all your festivals—I'm flesh and blood :—
Gems, dresses, ornaments, do little good;
You know full well, betwixt the head and heel,
Though little's said, yet much we often feel."
On this she stopped, and Richard dropped his chin,
Rejoiced to 'scape from such unwelcome din.

Bartholomea, pleased with what had passed,
No disposition showed to hold him fast ;
The downcast husband felt such poignant grief,
With ills where age can scarcely hope relief,
That soon he left this busy stage of life,
And Pagamin the widow took to wife.
The deed was just, for neither of the two
E'er felt what oft in Richard rose to view ;
From feeling proof arose their mutual choice,
And 'tween them ne'er was heard the jarring voice.

Behold a lesson for the aged man,
Who thinks, when old, to act as he began ;
But if the sage a yielding dotard seems,
His work is done by those the wife esteems ;
Complaints are never heard, no thrilling fears,
And every one around at ease appears.

THE AVARICIOUS WIFE AND
TRICKING GALLANT

WHO knows the world will never feel surprise,
　　When men are duped by artful women's eyes;
　　Though death his weapon freely will unfold,
Love's pranks, we find, are ever ruled by gold.
To vain coquettes I doubtless here allude;
But spite of arts with which they're oft endued,
I hope to show (our honour to maintain)
We can, among a hundred of the train,
Catch one at least, and play some cunning trick ;—
For instance, take blithe Gulphar's wily nick,
Who gained (old-soldier like) his ardent aim,
And gratis got an avaricious dame.

Look well at this, ye heroes of the sword,
Howe'er with wily freaks your heads be stored,
Beyond a doubt, at court I now could find
A host of lovers of the Gulphar kind.

To Gasperin's so often went our wight,
The wife at length became his sole delight,
Whose youth and beauty were by all confessed;
But, 'midst these charms, such avarice she possessed,

The warmest love was checked ;—a thing not rare,
In modern times at least, among the fair.
'Tis true, as I've already said, with such
Sighs nought avail, and promises not much ;
Without a purse, who wishes should express
Would vainly hope to gain a soft caress.
The God of Love no other charm employs
Than cards, and dress, and pleasure's cheering joys ;
From whose gay shops more cuckolds we behold
Than heroes sallied from Troy's horse of old.

But to our lady's humour let's adhere ;
Sighs passed for nought ; they entered not her ear ;
'Twas *speaking* only would the charmer please ;—
The reader, without doubt, my meaning sees.
Gay Gulphar plainly spoke, and named a sum—
A hundred pounds ; she listened—was o'ercome.

Our wight the cash by Gasperin was lent ;
And then the husband to the country went,
Without suspecting that his loving mate
Designed with horns to ornament his pate.

The money artful Gulphar gave the dame,
While friends were round who could observe the same.
" Here," said the spark, " a hundred pounds receive ;
'Tis for your spouse—the cash with you I leave."
The lady fancied what the swain had said
Was policy, and to concealment led.

Next morn our belle regaled the arch gallant,
Fulfilled her promise—and his eager want.

Day after day he followed up the game,
For cash he took, and int'rest on the same ;
Good payers get, we always may conclude,
Full measure served, whatever is pursued.

When Gasperin returned, our crafty wight
Before the wife addressed her spouse at sight ;
Said he, "The cash I've to your lady paid,
Not having (as I feared) required its aid ;
To save mistakes, pray cross it in your book."
The lady, thunderstruck, with terror shook,
Allowed the payment ; 'twas a case too clear ;
In truth, for character she 'gan to fear.
But most, howe'er, she grudged the surplus joy
Bestowed on such a vile, deceitful boy.

The loss was doubtless great in every view ;
Around the town the wicked Gulphar flew,
In all the streets, at every house to tell
How nicely he had tricked the greedy belle.

To blame him useless 'twere, you must allow ;
The French such frolics readily avow.

THE JEALOUS HUSBAND

A CERTAIN husband, who, from jealous fear,
With one eye slept, while t'other watched his dear,
Deprived his wife of every social joy
(Friends oft the jealous character annoy),
And made a fine collection in a book
Of tricks with which the sex their wishes hook.
Strange fool! as if their wiles, to speak the truth,
Were not a hydra, both in age and youth.

His wife, howe'er, engaged his constant cares;
He counted e'en the number of her hairs,
And kept a hag who followed every hour
Where'er she went, each motion to devour;
Duenna-like, true semblance of a shade,
That never quits, yet moves as if afraid.

This arch-collection, like a prayer-book bound,
Was in the blockhead's pocket always found;
The form religious of the work, he thought,
Would prove a charm 'gainst vice whenever sought.

One holy day it happened that our dame,
As from the neighb'ring church she homeward came,
And passed a house, some wight, concealed from view,
A basketful of filth upon her threw.

With anxious care apologies were made;
The lady, frightened by the frolic played,
Quite unsuspicious to the mansion went;
Her aged friend for other clothes she sent,
Who hurried home, and ent'ring out of breath,
Informed old hunks—what pained him more than death.

" Zounds !" cried the latter, " vainly I may look
To find a case like this within my book ;
A dupe I'm made, and nothing can be worse :—
Hell seize the work; 'tis thoroughly a curse !"

Not wrong he proved, for, truly to confess,
This throwing dirt upon the lady's dress
Was done to get the hag, with Argus' eyes,
Removed a certain distance from the prize.
The gay gallant, who watched the lucky hour,
Felt doubly blessed to have her in his power.

How vain our schemes to guard the wily sex !
Oft plots we find that every sense perplex.
Go, jealous husbands, books of cases burn ;
Caresses lavish, and you'll find return.

THE GASCON PUNISHED

A GASCON (being heard one day to swear
    That he'd possessed a certain lovely fair)
    Was played a wily trick and nicely served ;
'Twas clear from truth he shamefully had swerved.
But those who scandal propagate below
Are prophets thought, and every action know ;
While good, if spoken, scarcely is believed,
And must be viewed, or not for truth received.

The dame, indeed, the Gascon only jeered,
And e'er denied herself when he appeared ;
But when she met the wight, who sought to shine,
And called her angel, beauteous and divine,
She fled and hastened to a female friend,
Where she could laugh and at her ease unbend.

Near Phillis (our fair fugitive) there dwelled
One Eurilas, his nearest neighbour held ;
His wife was Cloris ;—'twas with her our dove
Took shelter from the Gascon's forward love,
Whose name was Dorilas ;—and Damon young
(The Gascon's friend), on whom gay Cloris hung.

Sweet Phillis, by her manner, you might see,
From sly amours and dark intrigues was free ;

The value to possess her no one knew,
Though all admired the lovely belle at view.
Just twenty years she counted at the time,
And now a widow was, though in her prime
(Her spouse, an aged dotard, worth a plum ;
Of those whose loss to mourn no tears e'er come).

Our seraph fair such loveliness possessed,
In num'rous ways a Gascon could have blessed ;
Above, below, appeared angelic charms ;
'Twas Paradise, 'twas Heaven, within her arms !

The Gascon was—a *Gascon ;*—would you more ?
Who knows one Gascon knows at least a score.
I need not say what solemn vows he made ;
Alike with Normans Gascons are portrayed ;
Their oaths, indeed, won't pass for Gospel truth,
But we believe that Dorilas (the youth)
Loved Phillis to his soul, our lady fair,
Yet he would fain be thought successful there.

One day said Phillis, with unusual glee,
Pretending with the Gascon to be free,
" A favour do me—nothing very great ;—
Assist to dupe one jealous of his mate.
You'll find it very easy to be done,
And doubtless 'twill produce a deal of fun.
'Tis our request (the plot, you'll say, is deep)
That you this night with Cloris' husband sleep.
Some disagreement with her gay gallant
Requires that she a night at least should grant,

To settle diff'rences; now we desire
That you'll to bed with Eurilas retire.
There's not a doubt he'll think his Cloris near;
He never touches her:—so nothing fear;
For, whether jealousy or other pains,
He constantly from intercourse abstains,
Snores through the night, and, if a cap he sees,
Believes his wife in bed, and feels at ease.
We'll properly equip you as a belle,
And I will certainly reward you well."

To gain but Phillis' smiles, the Gascon said
He'd with the very devil go to bed.

The night arrived, our wight the chamber traced;
The lights extinguished; Eurilas, too, placed;
The Gascon 'gan to tremble in a trice,
And soon with terror grew as cold as ice;
Durst neither spit nor cough, still less encroach,
And seemed to shrink, lest t'other should approach;
Crept near the edge, would scarcely room afford,
And could have passed the scabbard of a sword.

Oft in the night his bed-fellow turned round;
At length a finger on his nose he found,
Which Dorilas exceedingly distressed;
But more inquietude was in his breast,
For fear the husband amorous should grow,
From which incalculable ills might flow.

Our Gascon every minute knew alarm;
'Twas now a leg stretched out, and then an arm;

He even thought he felt the husband's beard;
But presently arrived what more he feared.

A bell, conveniently, was near the bed,
Which Eurilas to ring was often led;
At this the Gascon swooned, so great his fear,
And swore for ever he'd renounce his dear.
But no one coming, Eurilas once more
Resumed his place, and 'gan again to snore.

At length, before the sun his head had reared,
The door was opened and a torch appeared.
Misfortune then he fancied full in sight;
More pleased he'd been to rise without a light,
And clearly thought 'twas over with him now.
The flame approached;—the drops ran o'er his brow;
With terror he for pardon humbly prayed.
"You have it," cried a fair; "be not dismayed."
'Twas Phillis spoke, who Eurilas's place
Had filled throughout the night with wily grace,
And now to Damon and his Cloris flew,
With ridicule the Gascon to pursue;
Recounted all the terrors and affright
Which Dorilas had felt throughout the night.
To mortify still more the silly swain,
And fill his soul with every poignant pain,
She gave a glimpse of beauties to his view,
And from his presence instantly withdrew.

THE PRINCESS BETROTHED TO
THE KING OF GARBA

WHAT various ways in which a thing is told!
Some truth abuse, while others fiction hold;
In stories we invention may admit,
But diff'rent 'tis with what's historic writ;
Posterity demands that truth should then
Inspire relation and direct the pen.

Alaciel's story's of another kind,
And I've a little altered it, you'll find;
Faults some may see, and others disbelieve;
'Tis all the same—'twill never make me grieve.
Alaciel's mem'ry, it is very clear,
Can scarcely by it lose; there's nought to fear.
Two facts important I have kept in view,
In which the author fully I pursue;
The one—no less than eight the belle possessed
Before a husband's sight her eyes had blessed;
The other is, the prince she was to wed
Ne'er seemed to heed this trespass on his bed,
But thought, perhaps, the beauty she had got
Would prove to any one a happy lot.

Howe'er, this fair, amid adventures dire,
More sufferings shared than malice could desire;

Though eight times, doubtless, she exchanged her knight,
No proof that she her spouse was led to slight ;
'Twas gratitude, compassion, or goodwill ;
The dread of worse ;—she'd truly had her fill ;
Excuses just, to vindicate her fame,
Who, spite of troubles, fanned the monarch's flame.
Of eight the relict, still a maid received ;—
Apparently the prince her pure believed,
For, though at times we may be duped in this,
Yet, after such a number—strange to miss !
And I submit to those who've passed the scene,
If they to my opinion do not lean.

    The king of Alexandria, Zarus named,
A daughter had, who all his fondness claimed ;
A star divine Alaciel shone around,
The charms of beauty's queen were in her found ;
With soul celestial, gracious, good, and kind,
And all-accomplished, all-complying mind.

    The rumour of her worth spread far and wide,
The king of Garba asked her for his bride,
And Mamolin (the sov'reign of the spot)
To other princes had a pref'rence got.

    The fair, howe'er, already felt the smart
Of Cupid's arrow, and had lost her heart ;
But 'twas not known : princesses love conceal,
And scarcely dare its whispers fond reveal ;
Within their bosoms poignant pain remains,
Though flesh and blood, like lasses of the plains.

The noble Hispal, one of Zarus' court,
A handsome youth, as histories report,
Alaciel pleased; a mutual flame arose,
Though this they durst not venture to disclose;
Or, if expressed, 'twas solely by the eyes—
Soul-speaking language nothing can disguise!

Affianced thus, the princess, with a sigh,
Prepared to part, and fully to comply.
The father trusted her to Hispal's care,
Without the least suspicion of the snare;
They soon embarked and ploughed the briny main,
With anxious hopes in time the port to gain.

When they from Egypt's coast had sailed a week,
To gain the wind they saw a pirate seek,
Which having done, he t'wards them bore in haste,
To take the ship in which our fair was placed.

The battle quickly raged; alike they erred;
The pirates slaughter loved and blood preferred,
And, long accustomed to the stormy tide,
Were most expert, and on their skill relied.
In numbers, too, superior they were found;
But Hispal's valour greatly shone around,
And kept the combat undecided long.
At length Grifonio, wondrous large and strong,
With twenty sturdy pirates got on board,
And many soon lay gasping by the sword;
Where'er he trod grim death and horror reigned.
At length the round the noble Hispal gained;
His nervous arm laid many wretches low;
Rage marked his eyes whenc'er he dealt a blow.

But while the youth was thus engaged in fight,
Grifonio ran to gain a sweeter sight ;
The princess was on board full well he knew ;
No time he lost, but to her chamber flew ;
And since his pleasures seemed to be her doom,
He bore her like a sparrow from the room.
But not content with such a charming fair,
He took her diamonds, ornaments for hair,
And those dear pledges ladies oft receive
When they a lover's ardent flame believe.
Indeed, I've heard it hinted as a truth
(And very probable for such a youth)
That Hispal while on board his flame revealed ;
And what chagrin she felt was then concealed,
The passage thinking an improper time
To show a marked displeasure at his crime.

The pirate chief, who carried off his prey,
Had short-lived joy ; for, wishing to convey
His charming captive from the ship with speed,
One vessel chanced a little to recede,
Although securely fastened by the crew,
With grappling-hooks, as usually they do.
When quite intent to pass, young Hispal made
A blow, that dead at once the ruffian laid ;
His head and shoulders, severed from the trunk,
Fell in the sea, and to the bottom sunk,
Abjuring Mahomet and all the tribe
Of idle prophets Catholics proscribe.
Erect the rest upon the legs remained,
The very posture as before retained.

This curious sight no doubt a laugh had raised,
But in the moment she, so lately praised,
With dead Grifonio, fell beyond their view ;—
To save her straight the gallant Hispal flew.
The ships, for want of pilots at the helm,
At random drifted over Neptune's realm.

Grim death the pirate forced to quit his slave ;
Buoyed up by clothes, she floated on the wave,
Till Hispal succour lent, who saw 'twas vain
To try with her the vessel to regain.
He could, with greater ease, the fair convey
To certain rocks, and thither bent his way ;—
Those rocks to sailors oft destruction proved,
But now the couple saved, who thither moved.
'Tis even said the jewels were not lost,
But sweet Alaciel, howsoever tossed,
Preserved the caskets, which with strings were tied,
And seizing these, the treasure drew aside.

Our swimmer on his back the princess bore ;
The rock attained ; but hardships were not o'er ;
Misfortunes dire the noble pair pursued,
And famine, worst of ills, around was viewed.

No ship was near ; the light soon passed away ;
The night the same ; again appeared the day ;
No vessel hove in sight ; no food to eat ;
Our couple's wretchedness seemed now complete ;
Hope left them both, and, mutual passion moved,
Their situation more tormenting proved.

Long time in silence they each other eyed:
At length to speak the lovely charmer tried;
Said she, "'Tis useless, Hispal, to bewail:
Tears with the cruel Parcæ nought avail;
Each other to console be now our aim;
Grim Death his course will follow still the same.
To mitigate the smart let's try anew;
In such a place as this few joys accrue."

"Console each other, say you?" Hispal cried.
"What *can* console when forced one's love to hide?
Besides, fair princess, every way, 'tis clear,
Improper 'twere for you to love while here.
I equally could death or famine brave;
But you I tremble for, and wish to save."

These words so pained the fair that gushing tears
Bedewed Alaciel's cheeks; her looks spoke fears;
The ardent flame which she'd so long concealed
Burst forth in sighs, and all its warmth revealed;
While such emotion Hispal's eyes expressed
That more than words his anxious wish confessed.
These tender scenes were followed by a kiss,
The prelude sweet of soft enchanting bliss;
But whether taken or by choice bestowed,
Alike 'twas clear their heaving bosoms glowed.

"These vows now o'er," said Hispal, with a sigh,
"In this adventure, if we're doomed to die,
Indiff'rent surely 'tis the prey to be
Of birds of air or fishes of the sea.
My reason tells me every grave's the same;
Return we must, at last, from whence we came.

Here ling'ring death alone we can expect;
To brave the waves 'tis better to elect.
I yet have strength, and 'tis not far to land ;
The wind sets fair: let's try to gain the strand.
From rock to rock we'll go ; I many view
Where I can rest.   To this we'll bid adieu."

To move Alaciel readily agreed ;
Again our couple ventured to proceed.
The casket safe in tow, the weather hot,
From rock to rock with care our swimmer got,
The princess anxious on his back to keep—
New mode of traversing the wat'ry deep.

With Heaven's assistance, and the rocks for rest,
The youth, by hunger and fatigue oppressed,
Uneasiness of mind, weighed down with care,
Not for himself, but safety of the fair,
A fast of two long tedious days now o'er,
The casket and the belle he brought on shore.

I think you cry, " How wondrously exact,
To bring the casket into every act !
Is that a circumstance of weight, I pray ? "
It truly seems so, and without delay
You'll see if I be wrong; no airy flight,
Or jeer, or raillery have I in sight.
Had I embarked our couple in a ship
Without or cash or jewels for the trip,
Distress had followed, you must be aware ;
'Tis past our power to live on love or air ;
In vain affection every effort tries,
Inexorable hunger all defies.

The casket with the diamonds proved a source
To which 'twas requisite to have recourse;
Some Hispal sold, and others put in pawn,
And purchased, near the coast, a house and lawn,
With woods, extensive park, and pleasure-ground,
And many bowers and shady walks around,
Where charming hours they passed, and this, 'twas plain,
Without the casket they could ne'er obtain.

Beneath the wood there was a secret grot,
Where lovers, when they pleased, concealment got;
A quiet, gloomy, solitary place,
Designed by nature for the billing race.

One day, as through the grove a walk they sought,
The God of Love our couple thither brought;
His wishes Hispal, as they went along,
Explained in part by words direct and strong;
The rest his eyes expressed (they spoke the soul);—
The princess, trembling, listened to the whole.

Said he, " We now are in a place retired,
Unknown to man (such spots how oft desired)!
Let's take advantage of the present hour:
No joys but those of love are in our power;
All others see withdrawn; and no one knows
We even live; perhaps both friends and foes
Believe us in the belly of a whale;—
Allow me, lovely princess, to prevail;
Bestow your kindness, or, without delay,
Those charms to Mamolin let me convey.
Yet why go thither?—happy you could make
The man whose constancy no perils shake.

What would you more ?—his passion's ardent grown :
And surely you've enough resistance shown."

Such tender elocution Hispal used
That e'en to marble 'twould have warmth infused ;
While fair Alaciel on the bark of trees
With bodkin wrote, apparently at ease.
But Cupid drew her thoughts to higher things
Than merely graving what from fancy springs.
Her lover and the place at once assured
That such a secret would be well secured ;
A tempting bait, which made her, with regret,
Resist the witching charm that her beset.

Unluckily, 'twas then the month of May,
When youthful hearts are often led astray,
And soft desire can scarcely be concealed,
But presses through the pores to be revealed.

How many do we see, by slow degrees,
And step by step, accord their all to please,
Who, at the onset, never dreamed to grant
The smallest favour to their fond gallant !
The God of Love so archly acts his part,
And in unguarded moments melts the heart,
That many belles have tumbled in the snare,
Who how it happened scarcely could declare.

When they had reached the pleasing secret spot,
Young Hispal wished to go within the grot.
Though nearly overcome, she this declined ;
But then his services arose to mind ;

Her life from ocean's waves, her honour too,
To him she owed.   What could he have in view ?
A something which already has been shown
Was saved through Hispal's nervous arm alone.
Said he, " Far better bless a real friend
Than have each treasure rifled in the end
By some successful ruffian.   Think it o'er ;
You little dream for whom you guard the store."

The princess felt the truth of this remark,
And half surrendered to the loving spark.
A shower obliged the pair, without delay,
To seek a shed ;—the place I need not say.
The rest within the grotto lies concealed—
The scenes of Cupid ne'er should be revealed.
Alaciel blame, or not—I've many known,
With less excuses, who've like favours shown.

Alone the cavern witnessed not their bliss ;
In love, a point once gained, nought feels amiss ;
If trees could speak that grew within the dell,
What joys they viewed !—what stories they might tell !
The park, the lawn, the pleasure-grounds and bowers,
The belts of roses and the beds of flowers,
All, all could whisper something of the kind.
At length both longed their friends again to find ;
Quite cloyed with love, they sighed to be at court.
Thus spoke the fair her wishes to support :

" Loved youth, to me you must be ever dear ;
To doubt it would ungen'rous now appear ;
But tell me, pray, what's love without desire,
Devoid of fear, and nothing to acquire ?

Flame unconfined is soon exhausted found,
But, thwarted in its course, 'twill long abound ;
I fear this spot, which we so highly prize,
Will soon appear a desert in our eyes,
And prove at last our grave.   Relieve my woe ;
At once to Alexandria, Hispal, go ;
Alive pronounced, you presently will see
What worthy people think of you and me.
Conceal our residence, declare you came
My journey to prepare (your certain aim),
And see that I've a num'rous escort sent,
To guard me from a similar event.
By it, believe me, you shall nothing lose ;
And this is what I willingly would choose ;
For, be I single or in Hymen's band,
I'd have you follow me by sea and land ;
And be assured, should favour I withdraw,
That I've observed in you some glaring flaw."

Were her intentions fully as expressed,
Or contrary to what her lips confessed ?
No matter which her view, 'twas very plain,
If she would Hispal's services retain,
'Twere right the youth with promises to feed,
While his assistance she so much must need.

As soon as he was ready to depart
She pressed him fondly to her glowing heart,
And charged him with a letter to the king.
This Hispal hastened to the prince to bring ;
Each sail he crowded, plied with every oar ;
A wind quite fair soon brought him to the shore.

To court he went, where all, with eager eyes,
Demanded if he lived, amid surprise,
And where he left the princess; what her state.
These questions answered, Hispal, quite elate,
Procured the escort, which, without delay,
Though leaving him behind, was sent away.
No dark mistrust retained the noble youth;
But Zarus wished it: such appeared the truth.

By one of early years the troop was led,
A handsome lad, and elegantly bred.
He landed with his party near the park,
And these in two divided ere 'twas dark.
One half he left a guard upon the shore,
And with the other hastened to the door
Where dwelt the belle, who daily fairer grew.
Our chief was smitten instantly at view;
And, fearing opportunity again
Like this, perhaps, he never might obtain,
Avowed at once his passion to the fair.
At which she frowned, and told him, with an air,
To recollect his duty and her rank;—
With equals only he should be so frank.

On these occasions prudent 'tis to show
Your disappointment by a face of woe,
Seem every way the picture of despair.
This countenance our knight appeared to wear;
To starve himself he vowed was his design;
To use the poniard he should ne'er incline,
For then no time for penitence would rest.
The princess of his folly made a jest.

IIe fasted one whole day; she tried in vain
To make him from the enterprise refrain.

At length the second day she 'gan to feel,
And strong emotion scarcely could conceal.
What! let a person die her charms could save!
'Twas cruel thus to treat a youth so brave.
Through pity, she at last, to please the chief,
Consented to bestow on him relief;
For favours, when conferred with sullen air,
But little gratify, she was aware.

While satisfied the smart gallant appeared,
And anxiously to putting off adhered,
Pretending that the wind and tide would fail,
The galleys sometimes were unfit to sail,
Repairs required ;—then further heard the news
That certain pirates had unpleasant views ;
To fall upon the escort they'd contrived.
At length a pirate suddenly arrived,
Surprised the party left upon the shore,
Destroyed the whole ;—then sought the house for more,
And scaled the walls while darkness spread around.
The pirate was Grifonio's second found,
Who, in a trice, the noble mansion took,
And joy gave place to grief in every look.

The Alexandrian swore and cursed his lot ;
The pirate soon the lady's story got,
And, taking her aside, his share required.
Such impudence Alaciel's patience tired,
Who everything refused with haughty air.
Of this, howe'er, the robber was aware ;

In Venus' court no novice was he thought;
To gain the princess anxiously he sought.
Said he, " You'd better take me as a friend;
I'm more than pirate, and you'll comprehend,
As you've obliged one dying swain to fast,
You fast in turn, or you'll give way at last.
'Tis justice this demands: we sons of sea
Know how to deal with those of each degree;
Remember you will nothing have to eat
Till your surrender fully is complete.
No haggling, princess; pray, my word receive."
What could be done her terror to relieve?
Above all law is might;—'twill take its course;
Entire submission is the last resource.

   Oft what we would not we're obliged to do
When fate our steps with rigour will pursue;
No folly greater than to heighten pain
When we are sensible relief is vain.
What she, through pity, to another gave
Might well be granted when herself 'twould save.

   At length she yielded to this suitor rude—
No grief so great but what may be subdued.
'Twould in the pirate doubtless have been wise
The belle to move, and thus prevent surprise;
But who from folly in amours is free?
The God of Love and wisdom ne'er agree.

   While our gay pirate thought himself at ease,
The wind quite fair to sail when he might please,

Dame Fortune, sleepy only while we wake,
And slily watching when repose we take,
Contrived a trick the cunning knave to play,
And this was put in force ere break of day.

A lord, the owner of a neighb'ring seat,
Unmarried, fond of what was nice and neat,
Without attachment, and devoid of care,
Save something new to meet among the fair,
Grew tired of those he long around had viewed,
Now constantly, in thought, our belle pursued.
He'd money, friends, and credit all his days,
And could two thousand men at pleasure raise.
One charming morn together these he brought ;
Said he, " Brave fellows, can it well be thought
That we allow a pirate (dire disgrace !)
To plunder as he likes before our face,
And make a slave of one whose form's divine ?
Let's to the castle, such is my design,
And from the ruffian liberate the fair.
This evening every one will here repair,
Well armed, and then in silence we'll proceed
(By night 'tis likely nothing will impede),
And ere Aurora peeps perform the task.
The only booty that I mean to ask
Is this fair dame ;—but not a slave to make ;
I anxiously desire to let her take
Whate'er is hers :—restore her honour too.
All other things I freely leave to you,
Men, horses, baggage—in a word, the whole
Of what the knavish rascals now control.

Another thing, howe'er—I wish to hang
The pirate instantly, before his gang."

This speech so well succeeded to inspire
That scarcely could the men retain their ire.

The evening came, the party soon arrived;
They ate not much, but drink their rage revived.
By such expensive treats we've armies known
In Germany and Flanders overthrown;
And our commander was of this aware:—
'Twas prudent, surely, no expense to spare.

They carried ladders for the escalade,
And each was furnished with a tempered blade;
No other thing embarrassing they'd got;
No drums;—but all was silent as the grot.

They reached the house when nearly break of day,
The time old Morpheus' slumbers often weigh;
The gang, with few exceptions (then asleep),
Were sent their vigils with grim death to keep.

The chief hung up:—the princess soon appeared;
Her spirits presently our champion cheered.
The pirate scarcely had her bosom moved—
No tears at least a marked affection proved;
But by her prayers she pardon sought to gain
For some who were not in the conflict slain;
Consoled the dying, and lamented those
Who, by the sword, had closed their book of woes;
Then left the place without the least regret
Where such adventures and alarms she'd met.

'Tis said, indeed, she presently forgot
The two gallants who last became her lot ;
And I can easily the fact believe :
Removed from sight, but few for lovers grieve.

She by her neighbour was received, we're told,
'Mid costly furniture and burnished gold ;
We may suppose what splendour shone around
When all-attracting he would fain be found ;
The best of wines, each dish considered rare—
The gods themselves received not better fare.
Till then Alaciel ne'er had tasted wine ;
Her faith forbade a liquor so divine ;
And, unacquainted with the potent juice,
She much indulged at table in its use.
If lately love disquieted her brain,
New poison now pervaded every vein,
Both fraught with danger to the beauteous fair,
Whose charms should guarded be with every care.

The princess by the maids in bed was placed ;
Then thither went the host with anxious haste.
"What sought he ?" you will ask : "mere torpid charms."
I wish the like were clasped within my arms.
" Give me as much," said one the other week,
" And see if I'd a neighbour's kindness seek."
Through Morpheus' sleepy power and Bacchus' wine,
Our host at length completed his design.

Alaciel, when at morn she oped her eyes,
Was quite o'ercome with terror and surprise ;

No tears would flow, and fear restrained her voice ;
Unable to resist, she'd got no choice.

" A night thus passed," the wily lover said,
" Must surely give a licence to your bed."
The princess thought the same ; but our gallant,
Soon cloyed, for other conquests 'gan to pant.

The host one evening from the mansion went ;
A friend he left himself to represent,
And with the charming fair supply his place,
Which in the dark, he thought, with easy grace,
Might be effected if he held his tongue,
And properly behaved the whole night long.

To this the other willingly agreed
(What friend would be refused if thus in need ?)
And this new-comer had complete success ;
He scarcely could his ecstasy express.

The dame exclaimed, " Pray how could he pretend
To treat me so and leave me to a friend ? "
The other thought the host was much to blame ;
" But since 'tis o'er, " said he, " be now your aim
To punish his contempt of beauteous charms ;
With favours load me—take me to your arms ;
Caress with fond embrace, bestow delight,
And seem to love me, though in mere despite."

She followed his advice, avenged the wrong,
And nought omitted pleasures to prolong.
If he obtained his wishes from the fair,
The host about it scarcely seemed to care.

The sixth adventure of our charming belle
Some writers one way, some another, tell;
Whence many think that favour I have shown,
And for her, one gallant the less would own.
Mere scandal this;—from truth I would not swerve
To please the fair: more credence I deserve;
Her husband only eight precursors had;
The fact was such;—I none suppress nor add.

The host returned and found his friend content;
To pardon him Alaciel gave consent;
And 'tween them things would equally divide—
Of royal bosoms clemency's the pride.

While thus the princess passed from hand to hand,
She oft amused her fancy 'mong a band
Of charming belles that on her would attend,
And one of these she made an humble friend.
The fav'rite in the house a lover had,
A smart, engaging, handsome, clever lad,
Well-born, but much to violence inclined;
A wooer that could scarcely be confined
To gentle means, but oft his suit began
Where others end who follow Cupid's plan.

It one day happened that this forward spark
The girl we speak of met within the park,
And to a summer-house the fav'rite drew.
The course they took the princess chanced to view,
As wand'ring near; but neither swain nor fair
Suspicion had that any one was there;

And this gallant most confidently thought
The girl by force might to his terms be brought.
His wretched temper, obstacle to love,
And every bliss bestowed by heaven above,
Had oft his hopes of favours lately marred ;
And fear, with those designs, had also jarred.
The girl, howe'er, would likely have been kind,
If opportunities had pleased her mind.

The lover, now convinced that he was feared,
In dark designs upon her persevered.
No sooner had she entered than our·man
Locked instantly the door.   But vain his plan ;
To open it the princess had a key.
The girl her fault perceived, and tried to flee ;
He held her fast ; the charmer loudly called ;
The princess came—or vainly she had squalled.

Quite disappointed, overcome with ire,
He wholly lost respect amid desire,
And swore by all the gods that, ere they went,
The one or other should to him consent ;
Their hands he'd firmly tie to have his way ;
For help (the place so far) 'twere vain to pray.
To take a lot was all that he'd allow.
"Come, draw," he said ; "to Fortune you must bow.
No haggling, I request—comply ;—be still :
Resolved I am with one to have my will."

"What has the princess done ? " the girl replied,
"That you to make her suffer thus decide ? "
"Yes," said the spark, "if on her fall the lot,
Then you'll, at least for present, be forgot."

"No," cried Alaciel, "ne'er I'll have it said
To sacrifice I saw a maiden led;
I'll suffer rather all that you expect
If you will spare my friend as I direct."
'Twas all in vain; the lots were drawn at last,
And on the princess was the burthen cast.
The other was permitted to retire,
And each was sworn that nothing should transpire.
But our gallant would sooner have been hung
Than have upon such secrets held his tongue;
'Tis clear no longer silent he remained
Than one to listen to his tale he'd gained.

This change of favourites the princess grieved;
That Cupid trifled with her she perceived;
With much regret she saw her blooming charms
The Helen of too many Paris' arms.

One day it happened, as our beauteous belle
Was sleeping in a wood beside a dell,
By chance there passed, quite near, a wand'ring knight,
Like those the ladies followed with delight
When they on palfreys rode in days of old,
And purity were always thought to hold.

This knight, who copied those of famed romance,
Sir Roger, and the rest, in complaisance,
No sooner saw the princess thus asleep
Than instantly he wished a kiss to reap.
While thinking whether from the neck or lip
'Twere best the tempting balm of bliss to sip,
He suddenly began to recollect
The laws of chivalry he should respect.

Although the thought retained, his fervent prayer
To Cupid was, that while the nymph was there,
Her fascinating charms he might enjoy;
Sure love's soft scenes were ne'er designed to cloy!

The princess woke, and great surprise expressed.
"Oh, charming fair!" said he, "be not distressed;
No savage of the woods nor giant's nigh,
A wand'ring knight alone you now descry,
Delighted thus to meet a beauteous belle:
Such charms divine what angel can excel!"

This compliment was followed by his sighs,
And frank confession, both from tongue and eyes;
Our lover far in little time could go.
At length he offered on her to bestow
His hand and heart, and everything beside
Which custom sanctions when we seek a bride.

With courtesy his offer was received,
And she related what her bosom grieved;
Detailed her hist'ry, but with care concealed
The six gallants, as wrong to be revealed.
The knight in what he wished indulgence got;
And, while the princess much deplored her lot,
The youth proposed Alaciel he should bring
To Mamolin, or Alexandria's king.

"To Mamolin?" replied the princess fair.
"No, no;—I now indeed would fain repair
(Could I my wishes have) to Zarus' court,
My native country:—thither give support."

" If Cupid grant me life," rejoined the knight,
" You there shall go, and I'll assist your flight.
To have redress upon yourself depends,
As well as to requite the best of friends.
But should I perish in the bold design,
Submit you must, as wills the powers divine.
I'll freely say, howe'er, that I regard
My services enough to claim reward."

　　Alaciel readily to this agreed,
And favours fondly promised to concede ;
T' ensure, indeed, his guarding her throughout,
They were to be conferred upon the route,
From time to time as onward they should go ;
Not all at once, but daily some to flow.

　　Things thus arranged, the fair behind the knight
Got up at once, and with him took to flight.
Our cavalier his servants sought to find
That, when he crossed the wood, he left behind.
With these a nephew and his tutor rode ;
The belle a palfrey took, as more the mode ;
But by her walked attentively the spark.
A tale he'd now relate ; at times remark
The passing scene ; then press his ardent flame ;
And thus amused our royal, beauteous dame.

　　The treaty was most faithfully observed ;
No calculation wrong ; from nought they swerved.
At length they reached the sea ; on ship-board got,
A quick and pleasing passage was their lot,
Delightfully serene, which joy increased ;
To land they came (from perils thought released).

At Joppa they debarked; two days remained;
And when refreshed the proper road they gained;
Their escort was the lover's train alone.
On Asia's shores to plunder bands are prone;
By these were met our spark and lovely fair;
New dangers they, alas! were forced to share.

To cede, at first, their numbers forced the train;
But rallied by our knight they were again;
A desp'rate push he made, repulsed their force,
And by his valour stopped, at length, their course;
In which attack a mortal wound he got,
But was not left for dead upon the spot.

Before his death he full instructions gave
To grant the belle whatever she might crave;
He ordered, too, his nephew should convey
Alaciel to her home without delay,
Bequeathing him whatever he possessed,
And—what the princess owed among the rest.

At length, from dread alarms and tears released,
The pair fulfilled the will of our deceased;
Discharged each favour was, of which the last
Was cancelled just as they the frontiers passed.

The nephew here his precious charge resigned,
For fear the king should be displeased to find
His daughter guarded by a youthful swain;—
The tutor only with her could remain.

No words of mine, no language can express
The monarch's joy his child to repossess;

And, since the difficulty I perceive,
I'll imitate old Sol's retreat at eve,
Who falls with such rapidity of view,
He seems to plunge, dame Thetis to pursue.

The tutor liked his own details to hear,
And entertaining made his tales appear—
The num'rous perils that the fair had fled,
Who laughed aside, no doubt, at what he said.

"I should observe," the aged tutor cried,
"The princess, while for liberty she sighed,
And quite alone remained (by Hispal left),
That she might be of idleness bereft,
Resolved most fervently a god to serve,
From whom she scarcely since would ever swerve,
A god much worshipped 'mong the people there,
With num'rous temples which his honours share,
Denominated cabinets and bowers,
In which, from high respect to heavenly powers,
They represent the image of a bird,
A pleasing sight, though (what appears absurd)
'Tis bare of plumage, save about the wings;
To this each youthful bosom incense brings,
While other gods, as I've been often told,
They scarcely notice till they're growing old.
Did you but know the virtuous steps she trod,
While thus devoted to the little god,
You'd thank a hundred times the powers above
That gave you such a child to bless your love.
But many other customs there abound:—
The fair with perfect liberty are found:

Can go and come whene'er the humour fits;
No eunuch (shadow-like) that never quits,
But watches every movement, always feared;
No men but who've upon the chin a beard.
Your daughter, from the first, their manners took,
So easy is her every act and look;
And truly, to her honour, I may say
She's all-accommodating every way."

The king delighted seemed at what he heard;
But since her journey could not be deferred,
The princess, with a num'rous escort, tried
Again o'er seas t'wards Garba's shores to glide,
And there arrived, was cordially received
By Mamolin, who loved, she soon believed,
To fond excess; and, all her suite to aid,
A handsome gift to every one was made.

The king with noble feasts the court regaled,
At which Alaciel pleasantly detailed
Just what she liked; or true or false, 'twas clear,
The prince and courtiers were disposed to hear.

At night the queen retired to soft repose,
From whence next morn with honour she arose.
The king was found much pleasure to express;
Alaciel asked no more, you well may guess.

By this we learn that husbands who aver
Their wondrous penetration often err;
And while they fancy things so very plain,
They've been preceded by a fav'rite swain.

The safest rule's to be upon your guard,
Fear every guile, yet hope the full reward.

Sweet, charming fair, your characters revere ;
The Mamolin's a bird not common here.
With us love's fascination is so soon
Succeeded by the licensed honeymoon,
There's scarcely opportunity to fool,
Though oft the husband proves an easy tool.

Your friendships may be very chaste and pure,
But strangely Cupid's lessons will allure.
Defeat his wiles, resist his tempting charms ;
E'en from suspicion suffer not alarms.
Don't laugh at my advice ; 'twere like the boys,
Who better might amuse themselves with toys.

If any one, howe'er, unable seem
To make resistance 'gainst the flame supreme,
Turn all to jest ; though right to keep the crown,
Yet lost, 'twere wrong yourself to hang or drown.

THE MAGIC CUP

THE worst of ills with jealousy compared
Are trifling torments everywhere declared.

Imagine to yourself a silly fool
To dark suspicion grown an easy tool ;
No soft repose he finds by night or day,
But rings his ear, he's wretched every way !
Continually he dreams his forehead sprouts ;
The truth of reveries he never doubts.
But this I would not fully guarantee,
For he who dreams, 'tis said, asleep should be ;
And those who've caught, from time to time, a peep
Pretend to say the jealous never sleep.

A man who has suspicions soon will rouse ;
But buzz a fly around his precious spouse,
At once he fancies cuckoldom is brought,
And nothing can eradicate the thought ;
In spite of reason, he must have a place,
And numbered be, among the hornèd race ;
A cuckold to himself he freely owns,
Though otherwise perhaps in flesh and bones.

Good folks, of cuckoldom pray what's the harm,
To give, from time to time, such dire alarm ?

What injury's received and what's the wrong,
At which so many sneer and loll their tongue ?
While unacquainted with the fact, 'tis nought ;
If known, e'en then 'tis scarcely worth a thought.
You think, however, 'tis a serious grief ;
Then try to doubt it, which may bring relief,
And don't resemble him who took a sup
From out the celebrated magic cup.
Be warned by others' ills ; the tale I'll tell ;
Perhaps your irksomeness it may dispel.

But first, by reason let me prove, I pray,
That evil such as this, and which, you say,
Oft weighs you down with soul-corroding care,
Is only in the mind—mere sprite of air.
Your hat upon your head, for instance, place,
Less gently rather than's your usual case ;
Pray, don't it presently at ease remain ?
And from it do you aught amiss retain ?
Not e'en a spot ; there's nothing half so clear.
The features too, they as before appear ;
No difference assuredly you see ;
Then how can cuckoldom an evil be ?
Such my conclusion, spite of fools or brutes,
With whose ideas reason never suits.

"Yes, yes ; but honour has, you know, a claim."
Who e'er denied it ?—never 'twas my aim.
But what of honour ?—nothing else is heard ;
At Rome a diff'rent conduct is preferred.
The cuckold there who takes the thing to heart
Is thought a fool and acts a blockhead's part ;

While he who laughs is always well received,
And honest fellow through the town believed.
Were this misfortune viewed with proper eyes,
Such ills from cuckoldom would ne'er arise.

That advantageous 'tis we now will prove.
Folks laugh;—your wife a pliant glove shall move;
But if you've twenty favourites around,
A single syllable will ne'er resound.
Whenc'er you speak, each word has double force;
At table you've precedency of course,
And oft will get the very nicest parts,
Well pleased who serves you!—all the household smarts.
No means neglect your favour to obtain;
You've full command;—resistance would be vain.
Whence this conclusion must directly spring:
To be a cuckold is a useful thing.

At cards, should adverse fortune you pursue,
To take revenge is ever thought your due;
And your opponent often will revoke,
That you for better luck may have a cloak.
If you've a friend o'er head and ears in debt,
At once to help him numbers you can get.
You fancy these your rib regales and cheers:
She's better for't, more beautiful appears;
The Spartan king in Helen found new charms
When he'd recovered her from Paris' arms.
Your wife the same; to make her, in your eye,
More beautiful's the aim, you may rely;
For if unkind she would a hag be thought,
Incapable soft love-scenes to be taught.

These reasons make me to my thesis cling;—
To be a cuckold is a useful thing.

If much too long this introduction seem,
The obvious cause is clearly in the theme,
And should not certainly be hurried o'er.
But now for something from th' historic store.

A certain man, no matter for his name,
His country, rank, nor residence, nor fame,
Through fear of accidents had firmly sworn
The marriage chain by him should ne'er be worn ;
No tie but friendship from the sex he'd crave:
If wrong or right, the question we will waive.
Be this as 'twill, since Hymen could not find
Our wight to bear the wedded knot inclined,
The God of Love to manage for him tried,
And what he wished from time to time supplied.
A lively fair he got, who charms displayed,
And made him father to a little maid;
Then died, and left the spark dissolved in tears:
Not such as flow for wives (as oft appears),
When mourning's nothing more than change of dress:
His anguish spoke the soul in great distress.

The daughter grew in years, improved in mien,
And soon the woman in her air was seen.
Time rolls apace, and once a girl's her bib,
She alters daily, and her tongue gets glib ;
Each year still taller, till she's found at length
A perfect belle in look, in age, in strength.

His forward child, the father justly feared,
Would cheat the priest of fees so much revered ;
The lawyer too, and god of marriage joys ;
Sad fault, that future prospects oft destroys.
To trust her virtue was not quite so sure ;
He chose a convent, to be more secure,
Where this young charmer learned to pray and sew ;
No wicked books, unfit for girls to know,
Corruption's page the senses to beguile :
Dan Cupid never writes in convent style.

Of nothing would she talk but Holy Writ,
On which she could herself so well acquit
That oft the gravest teachers were confused.
To praise her beauty scarcely was excused ;
No flatt'ry pleasure gave, and she'd reply,
" Good sister, stay !—consider, we must die ;
Each feature perishes—'tis nought but clay,
And soon will worms upon our bodies prey."
Superior needlework our fair could do,
The spindle turn at ease, embroider too ;
Minerva's skill, or Clotho's, could impart ;
In tapestry she'd gained Arachne's art,
And other talents, too, the daughter showed ;
Her sense, wealth, beauty, soon were spread abroad.
But most her wealth a marked attention drew ;
The belle had been immured with prudent view,
To keep her safely till a spouse was found
Who with sufficient riches should abound.
From convents heiresses are often led
Directly to the altar to be wed.

Some time the father had the girl declared
His lawful child, who all his fondness shared;
As soon as she was free from convent walls,
Her taste at once was changed from books to balls.
Around Calista (such was named our fair)
A host of lovers showed attentive care;
Cits, courtiers, officers, the beau, the sage,
Adventurers of every rank and age.
From these Calista presently made choice
Of one for whom her father gave his voice;
A handsome lad, and thought good-humoured too:
Few otherwise appear when first they woo.
Her fortune ample was; the dower the same;
The belle an only child; the like her flame.
But better still, our couple's chief delight
Was mutual love and pleasure to excite.

Two years in paradise thus passed the pair,
When bliss was changed to hell's worst cank'ring care;
A fit of jealousy the husband grieved,
And, strange to tell, he all at once believed
A lover with success his wife addressed,
When but for him the suit had ne'er been pressed;
For though the spark the charming fair to gain
Would every wily method try, 'twas plain,
Yet had the husband never terrors shown,
The lover, in despair, had quickly flown.

What should a husband do whose wife is sought
With anxious fondness by another?   Nought.
'Tis this that leads me ever to advise
To sleep at ease, whichever side he lies.

In case she lends the spark a willing ear,
'Twill not be better if you interfere :
She'll seek more opportunities, you'll find ;
But if to pay attention she's inclined,
You'll raise the inclination in her brain,
And then the danger will begin again.

Where'er suspicion dwells, you may be sure,
To cuckoldom 'twill prove a place secure.
But Damon (such the husband's name), 'tis clear,
Thought otherwise, as we shall make appear.
He merits pity, and should be excused,
Since he by bad advice was much abused,
When, had he trusted to himself to guide,
He'd acted wisely ;—hear and you'll decide.

Th' enchantress Neria flourished in those days ;
E'en Circe she excelled in Satan's ways.
The storms she made obedient to her will,
And regulated with superior skill ;
In chains the destinies she kept around ;
The gentle zephyrs were her pages found ;
The winds, her lackeys, flew with rapid course,
Alert, but obstinate, with pow'rful force.

With all her art th' enchantress could not find
A charm to guard her 'gainst the urchin blind ;
Though she'd the power to stop the star of day,
She burned to gain a being formed of clay.
If merely a salute her wish had been,
She might have had it, easily was seen ;

But bliss unbounded clearly was her view,
And this with anxious ardour she'd pursue.
Though charms she had, still Damon would remain
To her who had his heart a faithful swain ;
In vain she sought the genial soft caress :
To Neria nought but friendship he'd express.
Like Damon husbands nowhere now are found,
And I'm not certain such were e'er on ground.
I rather fancy hist'ry is not here
What we would wish, since truth it don't revere.
I nothing in the hippogriff perceive,
Or lance enchanted, but we may believe ;
Yet this, I must confess, has raised surprise.
Howe'er, to pass it will perhaps suffice ;
I've many passed the same ;—in ancient days
Men diff'rent were from us—had other ways,
Unlike the present manners, we'll suppose,
Or history would other facts disclose.

    The am'rous Neria, to obtain her end,
Made use of philters, and would e'en descend
To every wily look and secret art
That could to him she loved her flame impart.
Our swain his marriage vow to this opposed,
At which th' enchantress much surprise disclosed.
" You doubtless fancy," she exclaimed one day,
" That your fidelity must worth display ;
But I should like to know if equal care
Calista takes to act upon the square.
Suppose your wife had got a smart gallant,
Would you refuse as much a fair to grant ?

And if Calista, careless of your fame,
Should carry to extremes a guilty flame,
Would you but half-way go?   I truly thought
By sturdy Hymen thus you'd not be caught.
Domestic joys should be to cits confined,
For none but such were scenes like those designed.
But as to you :—decline love's choice pursuit?
No anxious wish to taste forbidden fruit?
Though such you banish from your thoughts, I see,
A friend thereto I fain would have you be.
Come, make the trial ; you'll Calista find
Quite new again when to her arms resigned.
But let me tell you, though your wife be chaste,
Erastus to your mansion oft is traced."

"And do you think," cried Damon, with an air,
" Erastus visits as a lover there?
Too much he seems my friend to act a part
That proves the villain both in head and heart."

Said Neria, mortified at this reply,
" Though he's a friend on whom you may rely,
Calista beauty has, much worth the man
With smart address to execute his plan ;
And when we meet accomplishments so rare,
Few women but will tumble in the snare."

This conversation was by Damon felt :
A wife, brisk, young, and formed 'mid joys to melt ;
A man well versed in Cupid's wily way,
No courtier bolder of the present day,
Well-made and handsome, with attractive mind ;—
To what might happen was the husband blind?

Whoever trusts implicitly to friends
Too oft will find on shadows he depends.
Pray where's the devotee who could withstand
The tempting glimpse of charms that all command
Which first invite by halves, then bolder grow,
Till fascination spreads and bosoms glow?
Our Damon fancied this already done,
Or, at the best, might be too soon begun.
On these foundations gloomy views arose,
Chimeras dire, destructive of repose.

Th' enchantress presently a hint received
That those suspicions much the husband grieved;
And better to succeed and make him fret,
She told him of a thing 'mong witches met.
'Twas metamorphose-water (such the name);
With this could Damon take Erastus' frame,
His gait, his look, his carriage, air, and voice:
Thus changed, he easily could mark her choice,
Each step observe :—enough, he asked no more.
Erastus' shape the husband quickly bore;
His easy manner and appearance caught.
With captivating smiles his wife he sought,
And thus addressed the fair with every grace—
" How blithe that look !   Enchanting is your face;
Your beauty's always great, I needs must say,
But never more delightful than to-day."

Calista saw the flatt'ring lover's scheme,
And turned to ridicule the wily theme.
His manner Damon changed from gay to grave,
Now sighs, then tears; but nothing could enslave;

The lady virtue firmly would maintain.
At length the husband, seeing all was vain,
Proposed a bribe, and offered such a sum,
Her anger dropped: the belle was overcome.
The price was very large, it might excuse,
Though she at first was prompted to refuse.
At last, howe'er, her chastity gave way—
To gold's allurements few will offer nay!
The cash resistance had so fully laid,
Surrender would at any time be made.
The precious ore has universal charms,
Enchains the will, or sets the world in arms!

Though elegant your form and smart your dress,
Your air, your language, every warmth express,
Yet if a banker or a financier
With handsome presents happen to appear,
At once is blessed the wealthy paramour,
While you a year may languish at the door.

This heart inflexible, it seems, gave ground
To money's pow'rful, all-subduing sound;
The rock now disappeared, and in its stead
A lamb was found, quite easy to be led,
Who, as a proof resistance she would waive,
A kiss, by way of earnest, freely gave.

No further would the husband push the dame,
Nor be himself a witness of his shame,
But straight resumed his form, and to his wife,
Cried, " O Calista ! once my soul and life ;

Calista, whom I fondly cherished long;
Calista, whose affection was so strong,
Is gold more dear than hearts in union twined?
To wash thy guilt thy blood should be assigned.
But still I love thee, spite of evil thought;
My death will pay the ills thou'st on me brought."

The metamorphosis our dame surprised;
To give relief her tears but just sufficed;
She scarcely spoke.   The husband days remained
Reflecting on the circumstance that pained.
Himself a cuckold could he ever make,
By mere design a liberty to take?
But horned or not? the question seemed to be.
When Neria told him, if from doubts not free,
Drink from the cup; with so much art 'tis made,
That whosoe'er of cuckoldom's afraid,
Let him but put it to his eager lips—
If he's a cuckold out the liquor slips;
He nought can swallow, and the whole is thrown
About his face or clothes, as oft 's been shown.
But should from out his brow no horns yet pop,
He drinks the whole, nor spills a single drop.

The doubt to solve, our husband took a sup
From this famed, formidable magic cup;
Nor did he any of the liquor waste.
"Well, I am safe," said he; "my wife is chaste,
Though on myself it wholly could depend;
But from it what have I to apprehend?
Make room, good folks, who leafless branches wear,
If you desire those honours I should share."

Thus Damon spoke, and to his precious wife
A curious sermon preached, it seems, on life.

If cuckoldom, my friends, such torments give,
'Tis better far 'mong savages to live!

Lest worse should happen, Damon settled spies,
Who o'er his lady watched with Argus eyes.
She turned coquette; restraints the fair awake,
And only prompt more liberties to take.
The silly husband secrets tried to know,
And rather seemed to seek the wily foe,
Which fear has often rendered fatal round,
When otherwise the ill had ne'er been found.

Four times an hour his lips to sip he placed,
And clearly for a week was not disgraced.
Howe'er, no further went his ease of mind ;—
O fatal science! fatally designed!
With fury Damon threw the cup away,
And, in his rage, himself inclined to slay.

His wife he straight shut up within a tower,
Where, morn and night, he showed a husband's power,
Reproach bestowed ; while she bewailed her lot—
'Twere better far if he'd concealed the plot ;
For now from mouth to mouth and ear to ear
It echoed and re-echoed far and near.

Meanwhile Calista led a wretched life ;
No gold nor jewels Damon left his wife,
Which made the jailer faithful, since 'twere vain
To hope, unbribed, this Cerberus to gain.

At length the wife a lucky moment sought,
When Damon seemed by soft caresses caught.
Said she, "I've guilty been, I freely own;
But though my crime is great, I'm not alone.
Alas! how few escape from like mishap,
'Mong Hymen's band so common is the trap!
And though at you the immaculate may smile,
What use to fret and all the sex revile?"

"Well, I'll console myself, and pardon you,"
Cried Damon, "when sufficient I can view
Of ornamented foreheads, just like mine,
To form among themselves a royal line;
'Tis only to employ the magic cup,
From which I learned your secrets by a sup."

His plan to execute the husband went,
And every passenger was thither sent,
Where Damon entertained with sumptuous fare,
And at the end proposed the magic snare.
Said he, "My wife played truant to my bed;
Wish you to know if yours be e'er misled?
'Tis right how things go on at home to trace,
And if upon the cup your lips you place,
In case your wife be chaste there'll nought go wrong;
But if to Vulcan's troop you should belong,
And prove an antlered brother, you will spill
The liquor every way, in spite of skill."

To all the men that Damon could collect
The cup he offered, and they tried th' effect.

But few escaped, at which they laughed or cried,
As feelings led or cuckoldom they spied,
Whose surly countenance the wags believed
In many houses near might be perceived.

Already Damon had sufficient found
To form a regiment and march around.
At times they threatened governors to hang
Unless they would surrender to their gang;
But few they wanted to complete the force,
And soon a royal army made of course.
From day to day their numbers would augment,
Without the beat of drum to great extent;
Their rank was always fixed by length of horn:
Foot-soldiers those whose branches short were borne;
Dragoons, lieutenants, captains, some became,
And even colonels those of greater fame.
The portion spilled by each from out the vase
Was taken for the length, and fixed the place.
A wight who in an instant spilled the whole
Was made a gen'ral—not commander sole,
For many followed of the same degree,
And 'twas determined they should equals be.

The rank and file now nearly found complete,
And full enough an enemy to beat,
Young Reynold, nephew of famed Charlemain,
By chance came by: the spark they tried to gain,
And, after treating him with sumptuous cheer,
At length the magic cup was made·appear;
But no way Reynold could be led to drink.
" My wife," cried he, " I truly faithful think,

And that's enough; the cup can nothing more.
Should I, who sleep with two eyes, sleep with four?
I feel at ease, thank Heaven, and have no dread;
Then why to seek new cares should I be led?
Perhaps if I the cup should hold awry,
The liquor out might on a sudden fly;
I'm sometimes awkward, and in case the cup
Should fancy me another who would sup,
The error, doubtless, might unpleasant be:
To anything but this I will agree,
To give you pleasure, Damon; so adieu;"
Then Reynold from the antlered corps withdrew.

Said Damon, "Gentlemen, 'tis pretty clear
So wise as Reynold none of us appear;
But let's console ourselves;—'tis very plain,
The same are others:—to repine were vain."

At length such numbers on their rolls they bore,
Calista liberty obtained once more,
As promised formerly, and then her charms
Again were taken to her spouse's arms.

Let Reynold's conduct, husbands, be your line;
Who Damon's follows surely will repine.
Perhaps the first should have been made the chief;
Though, doubtless, that is matter of belief.
No mortal can from danger feel secure;
To be exempt from spilling who is sure?
Nor Roland, Reynold, nor famed Charlemain
But what had acted wrong to risk the stain.

THE FALCON

I RECOLLECT that lately much I blamed
The sort of lover avaricious named ;
  And if in opposites we reason see,
The liberal in Paradise should be.
The rule is just, and, with the warmest zeal,
To prove the fact I to the Church appeal.

  In Florence once there dwelt a gentle youth,
Who loved a certain beauteous belle with truth ;
O'er all his actions she had full control ;—
To please he would have sold his very soul.
If she amusements wished, he'd lavish gold,
Convinced in love or war you should be bold.
The cash ne'er spare ;—invincible its powers,
O'erturning walls or doors where'er it showers.
The precious ore can everything o'ercome ;
'Twill silence barking curs, make servants dumb ;
And these can render eloquent at will—
Excel e'en Tully in persuasive skill.
In short, he'd leave no quarter unsubdued,
Unless therein the fair he could include.
She stood th' attack, howe'er, and Frederick failed ;
His force was vain whenever he assailed ;

Without the least return his wealth he spent :
Lands, houses, manors of immense extent,
Were every now and then to auction brought ;
To gratify his love was all he thought.

The rank of squire till lately he had claimed
Now scarcely was he even Mister named.
Of wealth by Cupid's stratagems bereft,
A single farm was all the man had left ;
Friends very few, and such as God alone
Could tell if friendship they might not disown
The best were led their pity to express ;
'Twas all he got : it could not well be less.
To lend without security was wrong,
And former favours they'd forgotten long ;
With all that Frederick could or say or do,
His liberal conduct soon was lost to view.

With Clytia he no longer was received
Than while he was a man of wealth believed ;
Balls, concerts, op'ras, tournaments, and plays,
Expensive dresses, all engaging ways,
Were used to captivate this lady fair,
While scarcely one around but in despair,
Wife, widow, maid, his fond affection sought.
To gain him every wily art was brought ;
But all in vain :—by passion overpowered,
The belle, whose conduct others would have soured,
To him appeared a goddess full of charms,
Superior e'en to Helen, in his arms ;
From whence we may conclude the beauteous dame
Was always deaf to Frederick's ardent flame.

Enamoured of the belle, his lands he sold ;
The family estates were turned to gold ;
And many who the purchases had made,
With pelf accumulated by their trade,
Assumed the airs of men of noble birth—
Fair subjects oft for ridicule and mirth !

Rich Clytia was, and her good spouse, 'tis said,
Had lands which far and wide around were spread,
No cash nor presents she would ever take,
Yet suffered Frederick splendid treats to make,
Without designing recompense to grant,
Or being more than merely complaisant.

Already, if my mem'ry do not fail,
I've said the youth's estates were put to sale,
To pay for feasts the fair to entertain ;
And what he'd left was only one domain,
A petty farm, to which he now retired,
Ashamed to show where once so much admired ;
And wretched too, a prey to lorn despair,
Unable to obtain by splendid care
A beauty he'd pursued six years and more,
And should for ever fervently adore.
His want of merit was the cause, he thought,
That she could never to his wish be brought,
While from him not a syllable was heard
Against the lovely belle his soul preferred.

'Mid poverty oft Frederick sighed and wept ;
A toothless hag his only servant kept ;

His kitchen cold (where commonly he dwelled);
A pretty decent horse his stable held;
A falcon too; and round about the grange
Our quondam squire repeatedly would range,
Where oft to melancholy he was led
To sacrifice the game which near him fed;
By Clytia's cruelty the gun was seized,
And feathered victims black chagrin appeased.

'Twas thus the lover whiled his hours away;
His heartfelt torments nothing could allay,
Blessed if with fortune love he'd also lost,
Which constantly his earthly comforts crossed;
But this lorn passion preyed upon his mind—
Where'er he rode Black Care would mount behind.

Death took at length the husband of the fair.
An only son appointed was his heir,
A sickly child, whose life, 'twas pretty plain,
Could scarcely last till spring returned again,
Which made the husband, by his will, decree
His wife the infant's successor should be,
In case the babe at early years should die,
Who soon grew worse and raised the widow's sigh.

Too much affection parents ne'er can show—
A mother's feelings none but mothers know.

Fair Clytia round her child with anxious care
Watched day and night, and no expense would spare;

Inquired if this or that would please his taste ;
What he desired should be procured with haste ;
But nothing would he have that she proposed.
An ardent wish, howe'er, the boy disclosed,
For Frederick's falcon, and most anxious grew—
Tear followed tear, and nothing else would do.
When once a child has got a whim in brain,
No peace, no rest, till he the boon obtain.

We should observe our belle, near Frederick's cot,
A handsome house and many lands had got ;
'Twas there the lovely babe had lately heard
Most wondrous stories of the bird averred ;
No partridge e'er escaped its rapid wing—
On every morn down numbers it would bring.
No money for it would its owner take ;
Much grieved was Clytia such request to make.
The man, for her, of wealth had been bereft ;
How ask the only treasure he had left ?
And him if she were led to importune,
Could she expect that he 'd accord the boon ?
Alas ! ungratefully she oft repaid
His liberal treats, his concerts, serenade,
And haughtily behaved from first to last :
How be so bold (reflecting on the past)
To see the man that she so ill had used,
And ask a favour ?—could she be excused ?
But then her child !—perhaps his life 'twould save ;
Nought would he take ; the falcon she must crave.

That her sweet babe might be induced to eat,
She meant the bird of Frederick to entreat ;

Her boy was heard continually to cry,
Unless he had the falcon he should die.

These reasons strongly with the mother weighed;
Her visit to the squire was not delayed;
With fond affection for her darling heir,
One morn, alone, she sought the lorn repair.

To Frederick's eye an angel she appeared;
But shame he felt that she his soul revered
Should find him poor—no servants to attend,
Nor means to give a dinner to a friend.
The poverty in which he now was viewed
Distressed his mind and all his griefs renewed.
"Why come?" said he; "what led you thus to trace
An humble slave of your celestial face,
A villager, a wretched being here?
Too great the honour doubtless must appear;
'Twas somewhere else you surely meant to go."
The lady in a moment answered, "No."
Cried he, "I've neither cook nor kettle left;
Then how can I receive you, thus bereft?"
"But you have bread," said Clytia; "that will do."
The lover quickly to the poultry flew,
In search of eggs;—some bacon too he found;
But nothing else, except the hawk renowned,
Which caught his eye, and instantly was seized,
Slain, plucked, and made a fricassee that pleased.

Meanwhile the housekeeper for linen sought;
Knives, forks, plates, spoons, cups, glass, and chairs
  she brought;

The fricassee was served, the dame partook,
And on the dish with pleasure seemed to look.

    The dinner o'er, the widow then resolved
To ask the boon which in her mind revolved.
She thus began—" Good sir, you'll think me mad
To come and to your breast fresh trouble add ;
I've much to ask, and you will feel surprise
That one for whom your love could ne'er suffice
Should now request your celebrated bird.
Can I expect the grant ?   The thought's absurd.
But pardon, pray, a mother's anxious fear ;
'Tis for my child ;—his life to me is dear ;
The falcon solely can the infant save.
Yet since to you I nothing ever gave
For all your kindness oft on me bestowed—
Your fortune wasted ; e'en your nice abode,
Alas ! disposed of, large supplies to raise,
To entertain and please in various ways—
I cannot hope this falcon to obtain,
For sure I am the expectation's vain ;
No, rather perish child and mother too
Than such uneasiness should you pursue.
Allow, howe'er, this parent, I beseech,
Who loves her offspring 'yond the power of speech
Or language to express, her only boy,
Sole hope, sole comfort, all her earthly joy,
True mother like, to seek her child's relief,
And in your breast deposit now her grief.
Affection's power none better know than you,—
How few to love were ever half so true !

From such a bosom I may pardon crave :
Soft pity's ever with the good and brave ! "

"Alas !" the wretched lover straight replied,
" The bird was all I could for you provide ;
'Twas served for dinner."   " Dead !" exclaimed the
    dame,
While trembling terror overspread her frame.
" No jest," said he ; " and from the soul I wish
My heart, instead of that, had been the dish ;
But doomed, alas! am I by fate, 'tis clear,
To find no grace with her my soul holds dear.
I'd nothing left ; and when I saw the bird,
To kill it instantly the thought occurred ;
Those nought we grudge nor spare to entertain
Who o'er our feeling bosoms sov'reigns reign.
All I can do is speedily to get
Another falcon ; easily they're met ;
And by to-morrow I'll the bird procure."
" No, Fred'rick," she replied ; " I now conjure
You'll think no more about it ; what you've done
Is all that fondness could have shown a son ;
And whether fate has doomed the child to die,
Or with my prayers the powers above comply,
For you my gratitude will never end ;—
Pray let us hope to see you as a friend."

Then Clytia took her leave, and gave her hand—
A proof his love no more she would withstand.
He kissed and bathed her fingers with his tears ;
The second day grim death confirmed their fears.

The mourning lasted long and mother's grief,
But days and months at length bestowed relief;
No wretchedness so great, we may depend,
But what to Time's all-conq'ring scythe will bend.

Two famed physicians managed with such care
That they recovered her from wild despair,
And tears gave place to cheerfulness and joy;—
The one was Time, the other Venus' boy.
Her hand fair Clytia on the youth bestowed,
As much from love as what to him she owed.

Let not this instance, howsoe'er, mislead;
'Twere wrong with hope our fond desires to feed,
And waste our substance thus;—not all the fair
Possess of gratitude a decent share.
With this exception they appear divine;
In lovely woman angel charms combine.
The whole, indeed, I do not here include;
Alas! too many act the jilt and prude.
When kind, they're every blessing found below;
When otherwise, a curse we often know.

THE LITTLE DOG

THE key which opes the chest of hoarded gold
Unlocks the heart that favours would withhold.
To this the God of Love has oft recourse
When arrows fail to reach the secret source;
And I'll maintain he's right, for, 'mong mankind,
Nice presents everywhere we pleasing find;
Kings, princes, potentates, receive the same,
And when a lady thinks she's not to blame,
To do what custom tolerates around,
When Venus' acts are only Themis' found,
I'll nothing 'gainst her say; more faults than one,
Besides the present, have their course begun.

A Mantuan judge espoused a beauteous fair;
Her name was Argia;—Anselm was her care,
An aged dotard, trembling with alarms,
While she was young and blessed with seraph charms.
But, not content with such a pleasing prize,
His jealousy appeared without disguise,
Which greater admiration round her drew,
Who doubtless merited in every view
Attention from the first in rank or place,
So elegant her form, so fine her face.

'Twould endless prove, and nothing would avail,
Each lover's pain minutely to detail,
Their arts and wiles; enough 'twill be, no doubt,
To say the lady's heart was found so stout,
She let them sigh their precious hours away,
And scarcely seemed emotion to betray.

While at the judge's Cupid was employed,
Some weighty things the Mantuan state annoyed,
Of such importance that the rulers meant
An embassy should to the Pope be sent.
As Anselm was a judge of high degree,
No one so well ambassador could be.

'Twas with reluctance he agreed to go,
And be at Rome their mighty Plenipo';
The business would be long, and he must dwell
Six months or more abroad, he could not tell.
Though great the honour, he should leave his dove,
Which would be painful to connubial love.
Long embassies and journeys far from home
Oft cuckoldom around induce to roam.

The husband, full of fears about his wife,
Exclaimed, " My ever-darling, precious life,
I must away. Adieu! Be faithful, pray,
To one whose heart from you can never stray.
But swear to me, my duck (for, truth to tell,
I've reason to be jealous of my belle),
Now swear these sparks, whose ardour I perceive,
Have sighed without success, and I'll believe.

But still, your honour better to secure
From slander's tongue and virtue to ensure,
I'd have you to our country-house repair ;
The city quit ;—these sly gallants beware ;
Their presents too, accurst invention found,
With danger fraught, and ever much renowned ;
For always in the world where lovers move
These gifts the parent of assentment prove.
'Gainst those declare at once ; nor lend an ear
To flattery, their cunning sister-peer ;
If they approach, shut straight both ears and eyes,
For nothing you shall want that wealth supplies.
My store you may command ; the key behold,
Where I've deposited my notes and gold.
Receive my rents, expend whate'er you please ;
I'll look for no accounts ; live quite at ease.
I shall be satisfied with what you do,
If nought therein to raise a blush I view.
You've full permission to amuse your mind ;
Your love, howe'er, for me alone's designed ;
That, recollect, must be for my return,
For which our bosoms will with ardour burn."

The good man's bounty seemingly was sweet ;
All pleasures, one excepted, she might greet ;
But that, alas ! by bosoms unpossessed,
No happiness arises from the rest.

His lady promised everything required—
Deaf, blind, and cruel, whosoe'er admired ;
And not a present would her hand receive ;—
At his return, he fully might believe,

She would be found the same as when he went,
Without gallant or aught to discontent.

Her husband gone, she presently retired
Where Anselm had so earnestly desired.
The lovers came, but they were soon dismissed,
And told from visits they must all desist ;
Their assiduities were irksome grown,
And she was weary of their love-sick tone.
Save one, they all were odious to the fair ;
A handsome youth, with smart, engaging air ;
But whose attentions to the belle were vain ;
In spite of arts, his aim he could not gain.
His name was Atis, known to love and arms,
Who grudged no pains could he possess her charms.
Each wile he tried, and if he'd kept to sighs,
No doubt the source is one that never dries ;
But often diff'rent with expense 'tis found ;
His wealth was wasted rapidly around :
He wretched grew ; at length for debt he fled,
And sought a desert to conceal his head.

As on the road he moved a clown he met,
Who with his stick an adder tried to get
From out a thicket, where it hissing lay,
And hoped to drive the countryman away.
Our knight his object asked ; the clown replied,
" To slay the reptile anxiously I tried ;
Wherever met, an adder I would kill :
The race should be extinct if I'd my will."

" Why wouldst thou, friend," said Atis, "these destroy?
God meant that all should freely life enjoy."

The youthful knight for reptiles had, we find,
Less dread than what prevails with human-kind;
He bore them in his arms;—they marked his birth,
From noble Cadmus sprung, who, when on earth,
At last to serpent was in age transformed.
The adder's bush the clown no longer stormed,
No more the spotted reptile sought to stay,
But seized the time, and quickly crept away.

At length our lover to a wood retired;
To live concealed was what the youth desired;
Lorn silence reigned, except from birds that sang
And dells that oft with sweetest echo rang.
There happiness and frightful mis'ry lay
Quite undistinguished, classed with beasts of prey,
That growling prowled in search of food around:
There Atis consolation never found.
Love thither followed, and, however viewed,
'Twas vain to hope his passion to elude;
Retirement fed the tender, ardent flame,
And irksome every minute soon became.
"Let us return," cried he, "since such our fate:
'Tis better, Atis, bear her frowns and hate
Than of her beauteous features lose the view.
Ye nightingales and streams, ye woods, adieu!
When far from her I neither see nor hear,
'Tis she alone my senses still revere;
A slave I am, who fled her dire disdain,
Yet seek once more to wear the cruel chain."

As near some noble walls our knight arrived,
Which fairy hands to raise had once contrived,

His eyes beheld, at peep of early morn,
When bright Aurora's beams the earth adorn,
A beauteous nymph in royal robes attired,
Of noble mien and formed to be admired,
Who t'wards him drew, with pleasing, gracious air,
While he was wrapped in thought, a prey to care.
Said she, "I'd have you, Atis, happy be;
'Tis in my power, and this I hope to see.
A fairy greet me; Manto is my name;—
Your friend, and one you've served unknown—the same.
My fame you've heard, no doubt; from me proceeds
The Mantuan town, renowned for ancient deeds;
In days of yore I these foundations laid,
Which in duration equal I have made
To those of Memphis, where the Nile's proud course
Majestically flows from hidden source.
The cruel Parcæ are to us unknown;
We wondrous magic powers have often shown;
But wretched, spite of this, appears our lot:
Death never comes though various ills we've got,
For we to human maladies are prone,
And suffer greatly oft, I freely own.

"Once in each week to serpents we are changed;
Do you remember how you here arranged
To save an adder from a clown's attack?
'Twas I the furious rustic wished to hack
When you assisted me to get away;—
For recompense, my friend, without delay
I'll you procure the kindness of the fair,
Who makes you love and drives you to despair.

We'll go and see her ;—be assured from me
Before two days are past, as I foresee,
You'll gain by presents Argia and the rest
Who round her watch and are the suitor's pest.
Grudge no expense, be gen'rous, and be bold,
Your handfuls scatter, lavish be of gold,
Assured you shall not want the precious ore,
For I command the whole of Plutus' store,
Preserved, to please me, in the shades below ;
This charmer soon our magic power shall know.

" The better to approach the cruel belle,
And to your suit her prompt consent compel,
Myself transformed you'll presently perceive,
And, as a little dog, I'll much achieve.
Around and round I'll gambol o'er the lawn,
And every way attempt to please and fawn,
While you, a pilgrim, shall the bagpipe play ;
Come, bring me to the dame without delay."

No sooner said, the lover quickly changed,
Together with the fairy, as arranged ;
A pilgrim he, like Orpheus, piped and sang ;
While Manto, as a dog, skipped, jumped, and sprang.

They thus proceeded to the beauteous dame ;
Soon valets, maids, and others round them came.
The dog and pilgrim gave extreme delight,
And all were quite diverted at the sight.

.   The lady heard the noise, and sent her maid
To learn the reason why they romped and played.

She soon returned and told the lovely belle
A spaniel danced, and even spoke so well
It everything could fully understand,
And showed obedience to the least command.
'Twere better come herself and take a view:
The things were wondrous that the dog could do.

The dame at any price the dog would buy,
In case the master should the boon deny.
To give the dog our pilgrim was desired;
But though he would not grant the thing required,
He whispered to the maid the price he'd take,
And some proposals was induced to make.
Said he, "'Tis true the creature's not for sale;
Nor would I give it: prayers will ne'er prevail.
Whate'er I chance to want from day to day,
It furnishes without the least delay.
To have my wish three words alone I use,
Its paw I squeeze, and whatsoe'er I choose,
Of gold or jewels, fall upon the ground;
Search all the world, there's nothing like it found.
Your lady's rich, and money does not want;
Howe'er, my little dog to her I'll grant:
If she'll a night permit me in her bed,
The treasure shall at once to her be led."

The maid at this proposal felt surprise;
Her mistress, truly!   Less might well suffice.
"A paltry knave!" cried she; "it makes me laugh.
What! take within her bed a pilgrim's staff!
Were such a circumstance abroad to get,
My lady would with ridicule be met;

The dog and master probably were last
Beneath a hedge or on a dunghill cast;
A house like this they'll never see again."
But then the master is the pride of men,
And that in love is everything, we find;—
Much wealth and beauty please all womankind!

His features and his mien the knight had changed,
Each air and look for conquest were arranged.
The maid exclaimed, "When such a lover sues,
How can a woman anything refuse?
Besides, the pilgrim has a dog, 'tis plain,
Not all the wealth of China could obtain.
Yet to possess my lady for a night
Would to the master be supreme delight."

I should have mentioned that our cunning spark
The dog would whisper (feigning some remark),
On which ten ducats tumbled at his feet;
These Atis gave the maid (O deed discreet!).
Then fell a diamond: this our wily wight
Took up, and smiling at the precious sight,
Said he, "What now I hold I beg you'll bear
To her you serve, so worthy of your care;
Present my compliments, and to her say
I'm her devoted servant from to-day."

The female quickly to her mistress went,
Our charming little dog to represent:
The various powers displayed, and wonders done;
Yet scarcely had she on the knight begun,

And mentioned what he wished her to unfold,
But Argia could her rage no longer hold.
"A fellow! to presume," cried she, "to speak
Of me with freedom!   I am not so weak
To listen to such infamy, not I.
A pilgrim, too!—no, you may well rely,
E'en were he Atis, it would be the same,
To whom I now my cruel conduct blame;—
Such things he never would to me propose;
Not e'en a monarch would the like disclose;
I'm 'bove temptation; presents would not do;—
Not Plutus' stores if offered to my view.
A paltry pilgrim to presume, indeed,
To think that I would such a blackguard heed,
Ambassadress my rank! and to admit
A fellow only for the gallows fit!"

"This pilgrim," cried the maid, "has got the means
Not only belles to get, but even queens;
Or beauteous goddesses he could obtain;—
He's worth a thousand Atis's, 'tis plain."

"But," said the wife, "my husband made me vow."
"What!" cried the maid; "you'd not bedeck his brow!
A pretty promise, truly;—can you think
You less from this than from the first should shrink?
Who'll know the fact, or publish it around?
Consider well how many might be found
Who, were they marked with spot upon the nose,
When things had taken place that we suppose,
Would not their heads so very lofty place,
I'm well assured, but feel their own disgrace.

For such a thing are we the worse a hair ?
No, no, good lady ; who presumes to swear
He can discern the lips which have been pressed
By those that never have the fact confessed
Must be possessed of penetrating eyes,
Which pierce the sable veil of dark disguise.
This favour whether you accord or not,
'Twill not a whit be less nor more a blot.
For whom, I pray, love's treasures would you hoard ?
For one who never will a treat afford,
Or, what is much the same, has not the power ?
All he may want you'll give him in an hour
At his return ; he's very weak and old,
And, doubtless, every way is icy cold ! "

The cunning girl such rhetoric displayed
That all she said her mistress, having weighed,
Began to doubt alone, and not deny
The spaniel's art and pilgrim's piercing eye.
To her the master and his dog were led,
To satisfy her mind while still in bed ;
For bright Aurora, from the wat'ry deep,
Not more reluctantly arose from sleep.

Our spark approached the dame with easy air,
Which seemed the man of fashion to declare ;
His compliments were made with every grace
That minds most difficult could wish to trace.

The fair was charmed, and with him quite content ;
" You do not look," said she, " like one who meant

Saint James of Compostella soon to see,
Though, doubtless, oft to saints you bend the knee."

    To entertain the smiling, beauteous dame,
The dog, by various tricks, confirmed his flame;
To please the maid and mistress he'd in view:
Too much for these, of course, he could not do,
Though for the husband he would never move.
The little fav'rite sought again to prove
His wondrous worth, and scattered o'er the ground
With sudden shake, among the servants round,
Nice pearls, which they on strings arranged with care;
And these the pilgrim offered to the fair,
Gallantly fastened them around her arms,
Admired their whiteness and extolled her charms.
So well he managed, 'twas at length agreed
In what his heart desired he should succeed;
The dog was bought: the belle bestowed a kiss
As earnest of the promised future bliss.

    The night arrived, when Atis fondly pressed
Within his arms the lady thus caressed;
Himself he suddenly became again,
On which she scarcely could her joy contain;—
Th' ambassador she more respect should show
Than favours on a pilgrim to bestow.

    The fair and spark so much admired the night
That others followed equal in delight;
Each felt the same, for where's the perfect shade
That can conceal when joys like these pervade?
Expression strongly marks the youthful face,
And all that are not blind the truth can trace.

Some months had passed, when Anselm was dismissed ;
Of gifts and pardons long appeared his list ;
A load of honours from the Pope he got—
The Church will these most lib'rally allot.

From his vicegerent quickly he received
A good account, and friends his fears relieved ;
The servants never dropped a single word
Of what had passed, but all to please concurred.

The judge both maid and servants questioned much ;
But not a hint he got, their care was such.
Yet, as it often happens 'mong the fair,
The devil entered on a sudden there.
Such quarrels 'tween the maid and mistress rose,
The former vowed she would the tale disclose ;
Revenge induced her everything to tell,
Though she were implicated with the belle.

So great the husband's rage, no words can speak :
His fury somewhere he of course would wreak ;
But, since to paint it clearly would be vain,
You'll by the sequel judge his poignant pain.

A servant Anselm ordered to convey
His wife a note, who was, without delay,
To come to town her honoured spouse to see,
Extremely ill (for such he feigned to be).
As yet the lady in the country stayed ;
Her husband to and fro his visits paid.

Said he, " Remember, when upon the road,
Conducting Argia from her lone abode,

You must contrive her men to get away,
And with her none but you presume to stay.
A jade! she horns has planted on my brow ;—
Her death shall be the consequence, I vow.
With force a poniard in her bosom thrust ;
Watch well th' occasion ;—die, I say, she must.
The deed performed, escape ; here's for your aid ;
The money take ;—pursuit you can evade.
As I request proceed ; then trust to me ;—
You nought shall want wherever you may be."

To seek fair Argia instantly he went.
She, by her dog, was warned of his intent.
How these can warn? if asked, I shall reply,
They grumble, bark, complain, or fawn, or sigh ;
Pull petticoat or gown, and snarl at all
Who happen in their way just then to fall ;
But few so dull as not to comprehend.
Howe'er, this fav'rite whispered to his friend
The dangers that awaited her around ;
" But go," said he, " protection you have found ;
Confide in me ; I'll every ill prevent
For which the rascal hither has been sent."

As on they moved, a wood was in the way,
Where robbers often waited for their prey ;
The villain whom the husband had employed
Sent forward those whose company annoyed,
And would prevent his execrable plan ;
The last of horrid crimes—disgrace to man !
No sooner had the wretch his orders told
But Argia vanished ;—none could her behold ;

The beauteous belle was quickly lost to view :
A cloud the fairy Manto o'er her threw.

This circumstance astonished much the wretch,
Who ran to give our doting spouse a sketch
Of what had passed so strange upon the way.
Old Anselm thither went without delay,
When, marvellous to think ! with great surprise,
He saw a palace of extensive size
Erected where, an hour or two before,
A hovel was not seen, nor e'en a door.

The husband stood aghast—admired the place,
Not built for man ;—e'en gods 'twould not disgrace.
The rooms were gilt, the decorations fine,
The gardens and the pleasure-grounds divine ;
Such rich magnificence was never seen ;
Superb the whole, a charming blessed demesne.
The entrance every way was open found,
But not a person could be viewed around,
Except a negro, hideous to behold,
Who much resembled Æsop, famed of old.

Our judge the negro for a porter took,
Who was the house to clean and overlook ;
And taking him for such, the black addressed,
With full belief the title was the best,
And that he greatly honoured him, 'twas plain
(Of every colour men are proud and vain).
Said he, " My friend, what god this palace owns ?
Too much it seems for those of earthly thrones ;
No king of consequence enough could be."
" The palace," cried the black, " belongs to me."

The judge was instantly upon his knees,
The negro's pardon asked, and sought to please.
"I trust," said he, "my lord, you'll overlook
The fault I made: my ignorance mistook.
The universe has not so nice a spot,
The world so beautiful a palace got!"

"Dost wish me," said the black, "the house to give,
For thee and thine therein at ease to live?
On one condition thou shalt have the place:
For thee I seriously intend the grace,
If thou'lt on me a day or two attend
As page of honour;—dost thou comprehend?
The custom know'st thou?—better I'll expound;
A cup-bearer with Jupiter is found,
Thou'st heard, no doubt."

ANSELM

What, Ganymede?

NEGRO

The same;
And I'm that Jupiter of mighty fame,
The chief supreme who rules above the skies.
Be thou the lad with fascinating eyes,
Though not so handsome, nor, in truth, so young.

ANSELM

You jest, my lord; to youth I don't belong,
'Tis very clear;—my judge's dress—my age!

NEGRO

I jest ?   Thou dream'st.

ANSELM

My lord ?

NEGRO

You won't engage ?
Just as you will :—'tis all the same, you'll find.

ANSELM

My lord ! . . .

The learned judge himself resigned
The black's mysterious wishes to obey ;—
Alas ! curst presents, how they always weigh !

A page the magistrate was quickly seen,
In dress, in look, in age, in air, in mien ;
His hat became a cap ; his beard alone
Remained unchanged ; the rest had wholly flown.

Thus metamorphosed to a pretty boy,
The judge proceeded in the black's employ.
Within a corner hidden Argia lay,
And heard what Anselm had been led to say.
The Moor, howe'er, was Manto, most renowned,
Transformed, as oft the fairy we have found ;
She built the charming palace by her art ;—
Now youthful features would to age impart.

At length, as Anselm through a passage came,
He suddenly beheld his beauteous dame.

"What! learned Anselm do I see," said she,
"In this disguise? It surely cannot be;
My eyes deceive me;—Anselm, grave and wise,
Give such a lesson? I am all surprise.
'Tis doubtless he. Oh, oh! our bald-pate sire,
Ambassador and judge, we must admire
To see your honour thus in masquerade;—
At *your* age, truly, suffer to be made
A—modesty denies my tongue its powers.
What! *you* condemn to death for freaks like ours?
You, whom I've found * * * you understand;—for shame!
Your crimes are such as all must blush to name.
Though I may have a negro for gallant,
And erred when Atis for me seemed to pant,
His merit and the black's superior rank
Must lessen, if not quite excuse, my prank.
Howe'er, old boy, you presently shall see,
If any belle solicited should be
To grant indulgences with presents sweet,
She will not straight capitulation beat;
At least, if they be such as I have viewed.
Moor, change to dog." Immediately ensued
The metamorphose that the fair required;
The black'moor was again a dog admired.
"Dance, fav'rite." Instantly he skipped and played,
And to the judge his pretty paw conveyed.
"Spaniel, scatter gold." Presently there fell
Large sums of money, as the sound could tell.
"Such strong temptation who can e'er evade?
The dog a present to your wife was made.
Then show me, if you can, upon the earth
A queen, a princess, of the highest birth,

Who would not virtue presently concede,
If such excuses for it she could plead;
Particularly if the giver proved
A handsome lad that elegantly moved.
I, truly, for the spaniel was exchanged;
What you'd too much of, freely I arranged
To grant away, this jewel to obtain:
My value's nothing great, you think, 'tis plain;
And, surely, you'd have thought me very wrong,
When such a prize I met, to haggle long.
'Twas he this palace raised;—but I have done;
Remember, since you've yet a course to run,
Take care again how you command my death;
In spite of your designs I draw my breath.
Though none but Atis with me had success,
I now desire he may Lucretia bless,
And wish her to surrender up her charms
(Just like myself) to his extended arms.
If you approve, our peace at once is made;
If not—while I've this dog I'm not afraid,
But you defy: I dread nor swords nor bowl;
The little dog can warn me of the whole;
The jealous he confounds; be that no more;
Such folly hence determine to give o'er.
If you to put restraints on women choose,
You'll sooner far their fond affections lose."

     The whole our judge conceded;—could he less?
The secret of his recent change of dress
Was promised to be kept; and that unknown,
E'en cuckoldom again might there have flown.

Our couple mutual compensation made,
Then bade adieu to hill and dale and glade.

Some critic asks the handsome palace' fate;
I answer, "That, my friend, I shan't relate;
It disappeared, no matter how nor when.
Why put such questions ?—strict is not my pen."
"The little dog, pray what of that became ?"
"To serve the lover was his constant aim."
"And how was that ?" "You're troublesome, my friend :
The dog perhaps would more assistance lend ;
On new intrigues his master might be bent ;
With single conquest who was e'er content ?"

The fav'rite spaniel oft was missing found ;
But when the little rogue had gone his round,
He'd then return, as if from work relieved,
To her who first his services received.
His fondness into fervent friendship grew ;
As such gay Atis visited anew ;
He often came, but Argia was sincere,
And firmly to her vow would now adhere.
Old Anselm, too, had sworn by heaven above
No more to be suspicious of his love,
And, if he ever page became again,
To suffer punishment's severest pain.

THE EEL PIE

HOWEVER exquisite we beauty find,
It satiates sense and palls upon the mind.
Brown bread as well as white must be for me ;
My motto ever is—Variety.

That brisk brunette, with languid, sleepy eye,
Delights my fancy.   Can you tell me why ?
The reason's plain enough :—she's something new.
The other mistress, long within my view,
Though lily fair, with seraph features blessed,
No more emotion raises in my breast ;
Her heart assents, while mine reluctant proves.
Whence this diversity that in us moves ?
From hence it rises, to be plain and free,
My motto ever is—Variety.

The same, in other words, I've often said ;
'Tis right, at times, disguise with care to spread.
The maxim's good, and with it I agree ;
My motto ever is—Variety.

A certain spouse the same device had got,
Whose wife by all was thought a handsome lot.

His love, howe'er, was over very soon;
It lasted only through the honeymoon;
Possession had his passion quite destroyed—
In Hymen's bands too oft the lover's cloyed.

One 'mong his valets had a pretty wife;
The master was himself quite full of life,
And soon the charmer to his wishes drew,
With which the husband discontented grew,
And having caught them in the very fact,
He rang his mate the changes for the act;
Sad names he called her, howsoever just.
A silly blockhead! thus to raise a dust
For what in every town's so common found;
May we worse fortune never meet around!

He made the paramour a grave harangue:
"Don't others give," said he, "the poignant pang;
But every one allow to keep his own,
As God and reason oft to man have shown,
And recommended fully to observe.
You from it surely have not cause to swerve;
You cannot plead that you for beauty pine:
You've one at home who far surpasses mine.
No longer give yourself such trouble, pray:
You to my helpmate too much honour pay;
Such marked attentions she can ne'er require;
Let each of us alone his own admire.
To others' wells you never ought to go
While yours with sweets is found to overflow;
I willingly appeal to connoisseurs.
If Heaven had blessed me with such bliss as yours,

That, when I please, your lady I could take,
I would not for a queen such charms forsake.
But since we can't prevent what now is known,
I wish, good sir, contented with your own
(And 'tis, I hope, without offence I speak),
You'll favours from my wife no longer seek."

The master neither no nor yes replied,
But orders gave, his man they should provide
For dinner every day, what pleased his taste,
A pie of eels, which near him should be placed.

His appetite at first was wondrous great;
Again the second time as much he ate;
But when the third appeared he felt disgust,
And not another morsel down could thrust.
The valet fain would try a diff'rent dish;
'Twas not allowed;—"You've got," said they, "your
    wish;—
'Tis pie alone; you like it best, you know,
And no objection you must dare to show."

"I'm surfeited," cried he; "'tis far too much;
Pie every day, and nothing else to touch!
Not e'en a roasted eel, or stewed, or fried!
Dry bread I'd rather you'd for me provide.
Of yours allow me some at any rate.
Pies (devil take them!) thoroughly I hate;
They'll follow me to Paradise, I fear,
Or farther yet;—Heaven keep me from such cheer!"

Their noisy mirth the master thither drew,
Who much desired the frolic to pursue.

"My friend," said he, " I greatly feel surprised
That you so soon are weary grown of pies ;
Have I not heard you frequently declare
Eel pie's, of all, the most delicious fare ?
Quite fickle, certainly, must be your taste ;
Can anything in me so strange be traced ?
When I exchange a food which you admire,
You blame, and say I never ought to tire.
You do the very same.　In truth, my friend,
No mark of folly 'tis, you may depend,
In lord or squire, or citizen or clown,
To change the bread that's white for bit of brown.
With more experience you'll with me agree,—
My motto ever is—Variety."

When thus the master had himself expressed
The valet presently was less distressed.
Some arguments, howe'er, at first he used ;
For, after all, are fully we excused
When we our pleasure solely have in view,
Without regarding what's to others due ?
I relish change ;—well, take it ; but 'tis best
To gain the belles with love of gold possessed ;
And that appears to me the proper plan.
In truth, our lover very soon began
To practise this advice ;—his voice and way
Could angel-sweetness instantly convey.
His words were always gilt (impressive tongue !),
To gilded words will sure success belong.
In soft amours they're everything, 'tis plain ;
The maxim's certain, and our aim will gain.

My meaning doubtless easily is seen ;
A hundred times repeated this has been :
Th' impression should be made so very deep
That I thereon can never silence keep ;
And this the constant burden of my song—
To gilded words will sure success belong.

They easily persuade the beauteous dame,
Her dog, her maid, duenna, all the same ;
The husband sometimes too, and him we've shown
'Twas necessary here to gain alone.
By golden eloquence his soul was lulled,
Although from ancient orators not culled :
Their books retained have nothing of the kind.
Our jealous spouse indulgent grew, we find ;
He followed e'en, 'tis said, the other's plan,
And thence his dishes to exchange began.

The master and his fav'rite's freaks around
Continually the table-talk were found ;
He always thought the newest face the best :
Where'er he could each beauty he caressed ;
The wife, the widow, daughter, servant-maid,
The nymph of field or town—with all he played ;
And, while he breathed, the same would always be ;
His motto ever was—Variety.

THE MAGNIFICENT

SOME wit, handsome form, and generous mind
   A triple engine prove in love, we find;
     By these the strongest fortresses are gained ;
E'en rocks 'gainst such can never be sustained.
If you've some talents, with a pleasing face,
Your purse-strings open free, and you've the place.
At times, no doubt, without these things success
Attends the gay gallant, we must confess ;
But then good sense should o'er his actions rule ;
At all events he must not be a fool.
The stingy, women ever will detest ;
Words puppies want ;—the lib'ral are the best.

   A Florentine, Magnificent by name,
Was what we've just described, in fact and fame ;
The title was bestowed upon the knight
For noble deeds performed by him in fight.
The honour every way he well deserved :
His upright conduct (whence he never swerved),
Expensive equipage, and presents made,
Proclaimed him all around what we've portrayed.

   With handsome person and a pleasing mien,
Gallant, a polished air, and soul serene,

A certain fair of noble birth he sought,
Whose conquest, doubtless, brilliant would be thought
Which in our lover doubly raised desire ;
Renown and pleasure lent his bosom fire.

The jealous husband of the beauteous fair
Was Aldobrandin, whose suspicious care
Resembled more what frequently is shown
For fav'rite mistresses than wives alone.
He watched her every step with all his eyes ;
A hundred thousand scarcely would suffice ;
Indeed, quite useless Cupid these can make,
And Argus oft is subject to mistake :
Repeatedly they're duped, although our wight
(Who fancied he in everything was right)
Himself so perfectly secure believed,
By gay gallants he ne'er could be deceived.

To suitors, howsoe'er, he was not blind,
To covet presents greatly he inclined.
The lover yet had no occasion found
To drop a word to charms so much renowned ;
He thought his passion was not even seen ;
And if it had, would things have better been ?
What would have followed, what had been the end,
The reader needs no hint to comprehend.

But to return to our forlorn gallant,
Whose bosom for the lady's 'gan to pant ;
He to his doctor not a word had said ;
Now here, now there, he tried to pop his head.

But neither door nor window could he find
Where he might glimpse the object of his mind,
Or even hear her voice or sound her name ;
No fortress had he ever found the same.
Yet still to conquer he was quite resolved,
And oft the manner in his mind revolved.
This plan at length he thought would best succeed ;
To execute it doubtless he had need
Of every wily art he could devise,
Surrounded as he was by eagle eyes.

  I think the reader I've already told
Our husband loved rich presents to behold ;
Though none he made, yet all he would receive ;
Whate'er was offered he would never leave.

  Magnificent a handsome horse had got,
It ambled well, or cantered, or would trot ;
He greatly valued it, and for its pace
'Twas called the Pad ; it stepped with wondrous grace.
By Aldobrandin it was highly praised ;
Enough was this ;—the knight's fond hopes were raised,
Who offered to exchange ; but t'other thought
He in a barter might perhaps be caught.
"'Tis not," said he, " that I the horse refuse ;
But I, in trucking, never fail to lose."

  On this Magnificent, who saw his aim,
Replied, " Well, well, a better scheme we'll frame ;
No changing we'll allow, but you'll permit
That, for the horse, I with your lady sit,

You present all the while—'tis what I want ;
I'm curious, I confess, and for it pant.
Besides, your friends assuredly should know
What mind, what sentiments, may from her flow.
Just fifteen minutes, I no more desire."
"What !" cried the other; "you my wife require ?
No, no; pray keep your horse; that won't be right."
"But you'll be present," said the courteous knight.
"And what of that ?" rejoined the wily spouse.
"Why," cried Magnificent, "then nought should rouse
Your fears or cares, for how can ill arise,
While watched by you, possessed of eagle eyes ? "

    The husband 'gan to turn it in his mind;
Thought he, "If present, what can be designed ?
The plan is such as dissipates my fears;
The offer advantageous too appears.
He's surely mad; I can't conceive his aim;
But, to secure myself and wife from shame,
Without his knowledge, I'll forbid the fair
Her lips to open, and for this prepare."

    "Come," cried old Aldobrandin, "I'll consent."
"But," said the other, "recollect 'tis meant,
So distant from us all the while you stay,
That not a word you hear of what I say."
"Agreed," rejoined the husband; "let's begin."
Away he flew, and brought the lady in.

    When our gallant the charming belle perceived,
Elysium seemed around, he half believed.

The salutations o'er, they went and sat
Together in a corner, where their chat
Could not be heard, if they to talk inclined.
Our brisk gallant no long harangues designed,
But to the point advanced without delay ;
Cried he, " I've neither time nor place to say
What I could wish, and useless 'twere to seek
Expressions that but indirectly speak
The sentiments which animate the soul ;
In terms direct, 'tis better state the whole.
Thus circumstanced, fair lady, let me, pray,
To you at once my adoration pay ;
No words my admiration can express ;
Your charms enslave my senses, I confess.
Can you suppose to answer would be wrong ?
Too much good sense to you should now belong.
Had I the leisure, I'd in form disclose
The tender flame with which my bosom glows,
Each horrid torment ; but by fate denied
Blessed opportunities, let me not hide,
While moments offer, what pervades my heart,
And openly avow the burning smart :
Few minutes I have got to travel o'er
What gen'rally requires six months or more.
Cold is that lover who will not pursue,
With every ardour, beauty when in view.
But why this silence ?   Not a word you say !
You surely will not send me thus away !
That Heaven an angel made you none deny ;
But still to what is asked you should reply.
Your husband this contrived, I plainly see,
Who fancies that replies were not to be,

Since in our bargain they were never named ;
For shuffling conduct he was ever famed ;
But I'll come round him spite of all his art.
I can reply for you, and from the heart,
Since I can read your wishes in your eyes ;
'Tis thus you say, 'Good sir, I would advise
That you regard me not as marble cold ;
Your various tournaments and actions bold,
Your serenades, and gen'ral conduct prove
What tender sentiments your bosom move.
Your fond affection constantly I praised,
And quickly felt a flame within me raised ;
Yet what avails ? '—Oh, that I'll soon disclose ;
Since we agree, allow me to propose
Our mutual wishes we enjoy to-night,
And turn to ridicule that jealous wight ;
In short, reward him for his wily fear
In watching us so very closely here.
Your garden will be quite the thing, I guess ;
Go thither, pray, and never fear success.
Depend upon it, soon his country-seat
Your spouse will visit ;—then the hunks we'll cheat.
When plunged in sleep the grave duennas lie,
Arise, furred gown put on, and quickly fly ;
With careful steps you'll to the garden haste ;
I've got a ladder ready to be placed
Against the wall which joins your neighbour's square :
I've his permission thither to repair ;
'Tis better than the street ;—fear nought, my dove.
'Ah ! dear Magnificent, my fondest love,
As you desire, I'll readily proceed ;
My heart is yours : we fully are agreed.'

'Tis you who speaks, and would that in my arms
Permission I had got to clasp your charms!"

"'Magnificent' (for her he now replied),
"'This flame you'll soon no reason have to hide
Through dread or fear of my old jealous fool,
Who wisely fancies he can woman rule.'"

The lover, feigning rare, the lady left,
And grumbling much, as if of hope bereft,
Addressed the husband thus: "You're vastly kind;
As well with no one converse I might find;
If horses you so easily procure,
You fortune's frowns may very well endure.
Mine neighs at least, but this fair image seems
Mere pretty fish.   I've satisfied my schemes;
What now of precious minutes may remain,
If any one desire my chance to gain,
A bargain he shall have;—most cheap the prize."
The husband laughed till tears bedewed his eyes.
Said he, "These youths have always in their head
Some wondrous fancies; follies round them spread.
Friend, from pursuit you much too soon retire;
With time we oft obtain our fond desire.
But I shall always keep a watchful eye;
Some knowing tricks methinks I yet can spy.
Howe'er, the horse must now be clearly mine,
And you'll the Pad of course to me resign;
To you no more expense; and from to-day
Be not displeased to see me on it, pray;
At ease I'll ride my country-house to view."
That very night he to the mansion flew,

And our good folks immediately repaired,
Where gay Magnificent no pains had spared
To get access.   What passed we won't detail;
Soft scenes, you'll doubtless guess, should there prevail.

The dame was lively, beautiful, and young;
The lover handsome, finely formed, and strong;
Alike enchanted with each other's charms,
Three meetings were contrived without alarms;
A fair so captivating to possess,
What mortal could be satisfied with less?
In golden dreams the sage duennas slept;
A female sentinel to watch was kept.

A summer-house was at the garden end,
Which to the pair much ease was found to lend
Old Aldobrandin, when he built the same,
Ne'er fancied love would in it freak and game.
In cuckoldom he took his full degrees;
The horse he daily mounted at his ease,
And so delighted with his bargain seemed,
Three days to prove it requisite he deemed.
The country-house received him every night;
At home he never dreamed but all was right.

What numbers round, whom fortune favours less,
Have got a wife, but not a horse possess,
And, what yet still more wondrous may appear,
Know everything that passes with their dear!

THE EPHESIAN MATRON

IF there's a tale more common than the rest,
The one I mean to give is such confessed.
  "Why choose it, then?" you ask; "at whose desire?
Hast not enough already tuned thy lyre?
What favour can thy Matron now expect,
Since novelty thou clearly dost neglect?
Besides, thou'lt doubtless raise the critics' rage."
See if it looks more modern in my page.

At Ephesus, in former times, once shone
A fair whose charms would dignify a throne;
And, if to public rumour credit's due,
Celestial bliss her husband with her knew.
Nought else was talked of but her beauteous face,
And chastity that adds the highest grace;
From every quarter numbers flocked to see
This belle, regarded as from errors free,
The honour of her sex, and country too;
As such, old mothers held her up to view,
And wished their offspring's wives like her to act:
The sons desired the very same, in fact.
From her, beyond a doubt, our prudes descend,
An ancient, celebrated house, depend.

The spouse adored his beauteous, charming wife :
But soon, alas ! he lost his precious life.
'Twere useless on particulars to dwell ;
His testament, indeed, provided well
For her he loved on earth to fond excess,
Which 'yond a doubt, would have relieved distress,
Could gold a cherished husband's loss repair,
That filled her soul with black corroding care.

A widow, howsoever, oft appears
Distracted 'mid incessant floods of tears,
Who thoroughly her int'rest recollects,
And, spite of sobs, her property inspects.

Our Matron's cries were loudly heard around,
And feeling bosoms shuddered at the sound ;
Though we on these occasions truly know
The plaint is always greater than the woe.
Some ostentation ever is with grief :
Those who weep most the soonest gain relief.

Each friend endeavoured to console the fair ;
Of sorrow she'd already had her share :
'Twas wrong herself so fully to resign ;—
Such pious preachings only more incline
The soul to anguish 'mid distractions dire :
Extremes in everything will soonest tire.

At length, resolved to shun the glorious light,
Since her dear spouse no longer had the sight,
O'erwhelmed with grief, she sought Death's dreary cell,
Her love to follow, and with him to dwell.

A slave, through pity, with the widow went;
To live or die with her she was content.
To die, howe'er, she never could intend;
No doubt she only thought about her friend,
The mistress whom she never wished to quit,
Since from her birth with her she used to sit.
They loved each other with a friendship true:
From early years it daily stronger grew;
Look through the universe, you'll scarcely find
So great a likeness both in heart and mind.
The slave, more clever than the lady fair,
At first her mistress left to wild despair;
She then essayed to soothe each torment dire;
But reason's fruitless with a soul on fire.
No consolation would the belle receive;
For one no more she constantly would grieve,
And sought to follow him to regions blessed;—
The sword had shortest proved, if not the best.

But still the lady anxious was to view
Again those precious relics, and pursue
E'en in the tomb what yet her soul held dear.
No aliment she took her mind to cheer;
The gate of famine was the one she chose
By which to leave this nether world of woes.

A day she passed; another day the same;
Her only sustenance sobs, sighs, and flame;
Still unappeased, she murmured 'gainst her fate,
But nothing could her direful woes abate.

Another corpse a residence had got
A trifling distance from the gloomy spot;

But very diff'rent, since, by way of tomb,
Enchained on gibbet was the latter's doom;
To frighten robbers was the form designed,
And show the punishment that rogues should find.

A soldier as a sentinel was set
To guard the gallows, who good payment met.
'Twas ruled, howe'er, if robbers, parents, friends,
The body carried off, to make amends,
The sentinel at once should take its place;
Severity too great for such a case.
But public safety fully to maintain,
'Twas right the sentry pardon should not gain.

While moving round his post he saw at night
Shine 'cross the tomb a strange, unusual light,
Which thither drew him, curious to unfold
What through the chinks his eyesight could behold.

Our wight soon heard the lady's cries distressed,
On which he entered, and with ardour pressed
The cause of such excessive grief to know,
And if 'twas in his power to ease her woe.

Dissolved in tears and quite o'ercome with care,
She scarcely noticed that a man was there.
The corpse, howe'er, too plainly told her pain,
And fully seemed the myst'ry to explain.
"We've sworn," exclaimed the slave, "what's 'yond belief,
That here we'll die of famine and of grief."

Though eloquence was not the soldier's art,
He both convinced 'twas wrong with life to part.

The dame was great attention led to pay
To what the son of Mars inclined to say,
Which seemed to soften her severe distress:
With time each poignant smart is rendered less.

"If," said the soldier, "you have made a vow
That you some food to take will not allow,
Yet looking on while I my supper eat
Will not prolong your lives nor oaths defeat."

His open manner much was formed to please;
The lady and her maid grew more at ease,
Which made the gen'rous sentinel conclude
To bring his meat they would not fancy rude.

This done, the slave no longer was inclined
To follow Death, so soon she changed her mind.
Said she, "Good madam, pleasing thoughts I've got;
Don't you believe that, if you live or not,
'Tis to your husband every whit the same?
Had you gone first, would he have had the name
Of foll'wing to the grave as you design?
No, no; he'd to another course incline.
Long years of comfort we may clearly crave;
At twenty years it's surely wrong to brave
Both death and famine in a gloomy tomb:
There's time enough to think of such a doom.
At best, too soon we die;—do let us wait;
Here's nothing now at least to haste our fate.
In truth, I wish to see a good old age:
To bury charms like yours, would that be sage?
Of what advantage, I should wish to know,
To carry beauty to the shades below?

Those heavenly features make my bosom sigh,
To think from earthly praise they mean to fly."

This flatt'ry roused the beauteous widowed fair;
The god of soft persuasion soon was there,
And from his quiver in a moment drew
Two arrows keen, which from his bowstring flew;
With one he pierced the soldier to the heart,
The lady slightly felt the other dart.
Her youth and beauty, spite of tears, appeared,
And men of taste such charms had long revered;
A mind of tender feeling might through life
Have loved her—even though she were a wife.

The sentinel was smitten with her charms—
Grief, pity, sighs, belong to Cupid's arms;
When bosoms heave and eyes are drowned in tears,
Then beauty oft with conq'ring grace appears.

Behold our widow list'ning to his praise,
Incipient fuel Cupid's flame to raise;
Behold her even glad to view the wight,
Whose well-timed flatt'ry filled her with delight.

At length to eat he on the fair prevailed,
And pleased her better than the dead bewailed.
So well he managed that she changed her plan,
And, by degrees, to love him fondly 'gan.
The son of Mars a darling husband grew,
While yet her former dear was full in view.

Meantime the corpse, that long in chains had swung,
By thieves was carried off from where it hung.

The noise was heard, and thither ran our wight;
But vain his efforts—they were out of sight.
Confused, distressed, he sought again the tomb,
To tell his grief, and settle, 'mid the gloom,
How best to act and where his head to hide,
Since hang he must, the laws would now decide.

The slave replied, "Your gibbet-thief, you say,
Some lurking rogues this night have borne away.
The law, it seems, will ne'er accord you grace:
The corpse that's here let's set in t'other's place;
The passers-by the change will never tell."
The lady gave consent, and all was well.

O fickle females! ever you're the same;
A woman's woman both in mind and name!
Some fair we find and some unlike the dove,
But constancy's the highest charm of love.

Ye prudes, for ever doubt of full success;
Don't boast at all: too much you may profess.
How good soever your design may be,
Not less is ours, you easily may see;
The matron's tale is not beyond belief:
To entertain, our object is in chief.

The widow's only errors were her cries,
And mad design her life to sacrifice;
For merely setting husband-dead in place
Of one of this patibulary race

Was surely not a fault so very grave:
Her lover's life was what she sought to save.

A living drum-boy, truly be it said,
Is better far than any monarch dead.

BELPHEGOR

YOUR name with every pleasure here I place,
  The last effusions of my muse to grace.
    O charming Phillis! may the same extend
Through time's dark night: our praise together blend;
To this we surely may pretend to aim:
Your acting and my rhymes attention claim.
Long, long in mem'ry's page your fame shall live,
You, who such ecstasy so often give;
O'er minds, o'er hearts, triumphantly you reign;
In Berenice, in Phædra, and Chimene
Your tears and plaintive accents all engage;
Beyond compare in proud Camilla's rage;
Your voice and manner auditors delight;
Who strong emotions can so well excite?
No fine eulogium from my pen expect;
With you each air and grace appear correct.
My first of Phillises you ought to be;
My sole affection had been placed on thee
Long since had I presumed the truth to tell;
But he who loves would fain be loved as well.

No hope of gaining such a charming fair,
Too soon, perhaps, I ceded to despair;

Your friend was all I ventured to be thought,
Though in your net I more than half was caught.
Most willingly your lover I'd have been ;—
But time it is our story should be seen.

One day old Satan, sov'reign dread of hell,
Reviewed his subjects, as our hist'ries tell ;
The diff'rent ranks, confounded as they stood,
Kings, nobles, females, and plebeian blood,
Such grief expressed and made such horrid cries
As almost stunned, and filled him with surprise.
The monarch, as he passed, desired to know
The cause that sent each shade to realms below.
Some said, " My husband ; " others " Wife " replied ;
The same was echoed loud from every side.

His majesty on this was heard to say,
" If truth these shadows to my ears convey,
With ease our glory we may now augment :
I'm fully bent to try th' experiment.
With this design we must some demon send
Who wily art with prudence well can blend,
And, not content with watching Hymen's flock,
Must add his own experience to the stock."

The sable senate instantly approved
The proposition that the monarch moved.
Belphegor was to execute the work ;
The proper talent in him seemed to lurk :
All ears and eyes, a prying knave in grain ;
In short, the very thing they wished to gain.

That he might all expense and cost defray,
They gave him num'rous bills without delay,
And credit too, in every place of note,
With various things that might their plan promote.
He was, besides, the human lot to fill
Of pleasure and of pain, of good and ill ;
In fact, whate'er for mortals was designed,
With his legation was to be combined.
He might by industry and wily art
His own afflictions dissipate in part ;
But die he could not, nor his country see,
Till he ten years complete on earth should be.

Behold him trav'lling o'er th' extensive space
Between the realms of darkness and our race.
To pass it scarcely he a moment took ;
On Florence instantly he cast a look,
Delighted with the beauty of the spot,
He there resolved to fix his earthly lot,
Regarding it as proper for his wiles,
A city famed for wanton freaks and guiles.
Belphegor soon a noble mansion hired,
And furnished it with everything desired ;
As Signor Roderick he designed to pass ;
His equipage was large of every class,
Expense anticipating day by day,
What, in ten years, he had to throw away.

His noble entertainments raised surprise ;
Magnificence alone would not suffice ;
Delightful pleasures he dispensed around,
And flattery abundantly was found,

An art in which a demon should excel:
No devil surely e'er was liked so well.
His heart was soon the object of the fair;
To please Belphegor was their constant care.

Who lib'rally with presents smooths the road
Will meet no obstacles to Love's abode.
In every situation they are sweet,
I've often said, and now the same repeat.
The *primum mobile* of human kind
Are gold and silver through the world, we find.

Our envoy kept two books, in which he wrote
The names of all the married pairs of note;
But that assigned to couples satisfied,
He scarcely for it could a name provide,
Which made the demon almost blush to see
How few, alas! in wedlock's chains agree;
While presently the other, which contained
Th' unhappy—not a leaf in blank remained.

No other choice Belphegor now had got,
Than—try himself the hymeneal knot.
In Florence he beheld a certain fair,
With charming face, and smart, engaging air;
Of noble birth, but puffed up with empty pride;
Some marks of virtue, though not much beside.
For Roderick was asked this lofty dame.
The father said Honesta* (such her name)
Had many eligible offers found;

* By this character La Fontaine is supposed to have meant his own wife.

But, 'mong the num'rous band that hovered round,
Perhaps his daughter Rod'rick's suit might take,
Though he should wish for time the choice to make.
This approbation met, and Rod'rick 'gan
To use his arts and execute his plan.

    The entertainments, balls, and serenades,
Plays, concerts, presents, feats, and masquerades,
Much lessened what the demon with him brought ;
He nothing grudged ;—whate'er was wished he bought.
The dame believed high honour she bestowed
When she attention to his offer showed ;
And, after prayers, entreaties, and the rest,
To be his wife she full assent expressed.

    But first a pettifogger to him came,
Of whom (aside) Belphegor made a game.
"What!" said the demon; "is a lady gained
Just like a house ?   These scoundrels have obtained
Such power and sway, without them nothing's done ;
But hell will get them when their course is run."
He reasoned properly; when faith's no more,
True honesty is forced to leave the door ;
When men with confidence no longer view
Their fellow-mortals, happiness, adieu !
The very means we use t' escape the snare
Oft deeper plunge us in the gulf of care.
Avoid attorneys if you comfort crave,
Who knows a pettifogger knows a knave ;
Their contracts, filled with "ifs" and "fors," appear
The gate through which strife found admittance here.

In vain we hope again the earth 'twill leave ;
Still strife remains, and we ourselves deceive.
In spite of solemn forms and laws, we see
That Love and Hymen often disagree.
The heart alone can tranquillise the mind ;
In mutual passion every bliss we find.

How diff'rent things in other states appear !
With friends, 'tis who can be the most sincere ;
With lovers, all is sweetness, balm of life ;
While all is irksomeness with man and wife.
We daily see from duty springs disgust,
And pleasure likes true liberty to trust.

Are happy marriages for ever flown ?
On full consideration, I will own
That when each other's follies couples bear,
They then deserve the name of happy pair.

Enough of this ;—no sooner had our wight
The belle possessed, and passed the month's delight,
But he perceived what marriage must be here,
With such a demon in our nether sphere.
For ever jars and discords rang around ;
Of follies, every class our couple found.
Honesta oftentimes such noise would make,
Her screams and cries the neighbours kept awake,
Who, running thither, by the wife were told,
"Some paltry tradesman's daughter, coarse and bold,
He should have had ; not one of rank like me ;—
To treat me thus, what villain he must be !

A wife so virtuous could he e'er deserve?
My scruples are too great, or I should swerve;
Indeed, without dispute, 'twould serve him right."
We are not sure she nothing did in spite;
These prudes can make us credit what they please:
Few ponder long when they can dupe with ease.

This wife and husband, as our hist'ries say,
Each moment squabbled through the passing day;
Their disagreements often would arise
About a petticoat, cards, tables, pies,
Gowns, chairs, dice, summer-houses—in a word,
Things most ridiculous and quite absurd.

Well might this spouse regret his hell profound,
When he considered what he'd met on ground.
To make our demon's wretchedness complete,
Honesta's relatives, from every street,
He seemed to marry, since he daily fed
The father, mother, sister (fit to wed),
And little brother, whom he sent to school;
While Miss he portioned to a wealthy fool.

His utter ruin, howsoe'er, arose
From his attorney-steward that he chose.
"What's that?" you ask.   A wily, sneaking knave,
Who, while his master spends, contrives to save,
Till, in the end, grown rich, the lands he buys
Which his good lord is forced to sacrifice.

If, in a course of time, the master take
The place of steward, and his fortune make,

'Twould only to their proper rank restore
Those who become just what they were before.

Poor Rod'rick now no other hope had got
Than what the chance of traffic might allot ;
Illusion vain, or doubtful at the best ;—
Though some grow rich, yet all are not so blessed.
'Twas said our husband never would succeed,
And truly such it seemed to be decreed.
His agents (similar to those we see
In modern days) were with his treasure free ;
His ships were wrecked, his commerce came to nought ;
Deceived by knaves, of whom he well had thought,
Obliged to borrow money, which to pay
He was unable at th' appointed day,
He fled, and with a farmer shelter took,
Where he might hope the bailiffs would not look.

He told to Matthew (such the farmer's name)
His situation, character, and fame :
By duns assailed, and harassed by a wife
Who proved the very torment of his life,
He knew no place of safety to obtain
Like ent'ring other bodies, where, 'twas plain,
He might escape the catchpoll's prowling eye,
Honesta's wrath, and all her rage defy.
From these he promised he would thrice retire
Whenever Matthew should the same desire ;—
Thrice, but no more, t'oblige this worthy man,
Who shelter gave when from the fiends he ran.

Th' ambassador commenced his form to change ;—
From human frame to frame he 'gan to range ;

But what became his own fantastic state,
Our books are silent, nor the facts relate.

An only daughter was the first he seized,
Whose charms corporeal much our demon pleased ;
But Matthew, for a handsome sum of gold,
Obliged him, at a word, to quit his hold.
This passed at Naples.   Next to Rome he came,
Where with another fair he did the same ;
But still the farmer banished him again,
So well he could the devil's will restrain.
Another weighty purse to him was paid ;—
Thrice Matthew drove him out from belle and maid.

The king of Naples had a daughter fair,
Admired, adored, her parents' darling care ;
In wedlock oft by many princes sought.
Within her form, the wily demon thought,
He might be sheltered from Honesta's rage,
And none to drive him thence would dare engage.

Nought else was talked of, in or out of town,
But devils driven by the cunning clown ;
Large sums were offered if, by any art,
He'd make the demon from the fair depart.

Afflicted much was Matthew now to lose
The gold thus tendered, but he could not choose ;
For, since Belphegor had obliged him thrice,
He durst not hope the demon to entice ;
Poor man was he, a sinner, who, by chance
(He knew not how, it surely was romance),

Had some few devils, truly, driven out:
Most worthy of contempt, without a doubt.
But all in vain; the man they took by force;—
Proceed he must, or hanged he'd be, of course.

The demon was before our farmer placed;
The sight was by the prince in person graced;
The wondrous contest numbers ran to see,
And all the world spectators fain would be.

If vanquished by the devil—he must swing;
If vanquisher—'twould thousands to him bring.
The gallows was, no doubt, a horrid view,
Yet at the purse his glances often flew;
The evil spirit laughed within his sleeve
To see the farmer tremble, fret, and grieve;
He pleaded that the wight he'd thrice obeyed.
The demon was by Matthew often prayed,
But all in vain,—the more he terror showed,
The more Belphegor ridicule bestowed.

At length the clown was driven to declare
The fiend he was unable to ensnare;
Away they Matthew to the gallows led;
But as he went it entered in his head,
And, in a sort of whisper, he averred
(As was in fact the case) a drum he heard.

The demon, with surprise, to Matthew cried,
"What noise is that?" "Honesta," he replied,
"Who you demands, and everywhere pursues
The spouse who treats her with such vile abuse."

These words were thunder to Belphegor's ears,
Who instantly took flight, so great his fears;
To hell's abyss he fled without delay,
To tell adventures through the realms of day.
"Sire," said the demon, "it is clearly true
Damnation does the marriage-knot pursue.
Your highness often hither sees arrive,
Not squads, but regiments, who, when alive,
By Hymen were indissolubly tied;—
In person I the fact have fully tried.
Th' institution, perhaps, most just could be,
Past ages far more happiness might see;
But everything with time corruption shows—
No jewel in your crown more lustre throws."

Belphegor's tale by Satan was believed;
Reward he got: the term, which sorely grieved,
Was now reduced;—indeed, what had he done
That should prevent it?   If away he'd run,
Who would not do the same who weds a shrew?
Sure worse below the devil never knew!
A brawling woman's tongue what saint can bear?
E'en Job, Honesta would have taught despair.

"What is the inference?" you ask.   I'll tell;—
Live single, if you know when you are well;
But if old Hymen o'er your senses reign,
Beware Honestas, or you'll rue the chain.

THE LITTLE BELL

HOW weak is man! how changeable his mind!
His promises are nought, too oft we find.
I vowed (I hope in tolerable verse)
Again no idle story to rehearse.
And when this promise?   Not two days ago;
I'm quite confounded;—better I should know.
A rhymer hear, then, who himself can boast
Quite steady for—a minute at the most.
The powers above could prudence ne'er design
For those who fondly court the sisters nine.
Some means to please they've got, you will confess;
But none with certainty the charm possess.
If, howsoever, I were doomed to find
Such lines as fully would content the mind,
Though I should fail in matter, still in art
I might contrive some pleasure to impart.

Let's see what we are able to obtain:
A bachelor resided in Touraine,
A sprightly youth, who oft the maids beset,
And liked to prattle to the girls he met,
With sparkling eyes, white teeth, and easy air,
Plain russet petticoat and flowing hair,

Beside a rivulet, while Io round,
With little bell that gave a tinkling sound,
On herbs her palate gratified at will,
And grazed and played, and fondly took her fill.

Among the rustic nymphs our spark perceived
A charming girl, for whom his bosom heaved;
Too young, howe'er, to feel the poignant smart
By Cupid oft inflicted on the heart.
I will not say thirteen's an age unfit:
The contrary most fully I admit;
The law supposes (such its prudent fears)
Maturity at still more early years;
But this apparently refers to towns,
While love was born for groves, and lawns, and downs.

The youth exerted every art to please,
But all in vain; he only seemed to tease:
Whate'er he said, however nicely graced,
Ill-humour, inexperience, or distaste
Induced the belle, unlearned in Cupid's book,
To treat his passion with a froward look.

Believing every artifice in love
Was tolerated by the powers above,
One eve he turned a heifer from the rest,
Conducted by the girl his thoughts possessed;
The others left, not counted by the fair
(Youth seldom shows the necessary care),
With easy, loit'ring steps the cottage sought,
Where every night they usually were brought.

Her mother, more experienced than the maid,
Observed that from the cattle one had strayed.
The girl was scolded much, and sent to find
The heifer indiscreetly left behind.
Fair Isabella gave a vent to tears,
Invoked sweet Echo to disperse her fears,
Solicited with fervent, piercing cry
To tell her where lorn Io she might spy,
Whose little bell the spark deprived of sound
When he withdrew her from the herd around.

The lover now the tinkling metal shook ;
The path that t'wards it led the charmer took.
The well-known note was pleasing to her ear ;
Without suspecting treachery was near,
She followed to a wood both deep and large,
In hopes at least she might regain her charge.

Guess her surprise, good reader, when she heard
A lover's voice, who would not be deterred.
Said he, " Fair maid, whene'er the heart's on fire,
'Tis all permitted that can quench desire."
On this with piercing cries she rent the air,
But no one came ;—she sank to dire despair.

Ye beauteous dames, avoid the sylvan shade ;
Dread dangers solitary woods pervade.

THE GLUTTON

A STURGEON once a glutton famed was led
To have for supper—all except the head.
With wondrous glee he feasted on the fish,
And quickly swallowed down the royal dish.
O'ercharged, howe'er, his stomach soon gave way,
And doctors were required without delay.

The danger imminent, his friends desired
He'd settle everything affairs required.
Said he, " In that respect I'm quite prepared ;
And, since my time so little is declared,
With diligence, I earnestly request,
The sturgeon's head you'll get me nicely dressed."

THE TWO FRIENDS

AXIOCHUS, a handsome youth of old,
    And Alcibiades (both gay and bold)
        So well agreed, they kept a beauteous belle,
With whom by turns they equally would dwell.

It happened one of them so nicely played,
The fav'rite lass produced a little maid,
Which both extolled, and each his own believed,
Though doubtless one or t'other was deceived.

But when to riper years the bantling grew,
And sought her mother's footsteps to pursue,
Each friend desired to be her chosen swain,
And neither would a parent's name retain.

Said one, "Why, brother, she's your very shade;
The features are the same;—your looks pervade."
"Oh no," the other cried, "it cannot be;
Her chin, mouth, nose, and eyes with yours agree;
But that as 'twill, let me her favours win,
And for the pleasure I will risk the sin."

THE COUNTRY JUSTICE

TWO lawyers to their cause so well adhered,
   A country justice quite confused appeared;
   By them the facts were rendered so obscure,
With which the truth remained he was not sure.
At length, completely tired, two straws he sought
Of diff'rent lengths, and to the parties brought.
These in his hand he held;—the plaintiff drew
(So fate decreed) the shortest of the two.
On this the other homeward took his way,
To boast how nicely he had gained the day.

   The bench complained; the magistrate replied:
"Don't blame, I pray—'tis nothing new I've tried;
Courts often judge at hazard in the law,
Without deciding by the longest straw."

ALICE SICK

SICK, Alice grown, and fearing dire event,
Some friend advised a servant should be sent
Her confessor to bring and ease her mind.
"Yes," she replied, "to see him I'm inclined ;
Let Father Andrew instantly be sought—
By him salvation usually I'm taught."

A messenger was told, without delay,
To take, with rapid steps, the convent way.
He rang the bell ;—a monk inquired his name,
And asked for what, or whom, the fellow came.
" I Father Andrew want," the wight replied,
" Who's oft to Alice confessor and guide."
" With Andrew," cried the other, " would you speak ?
If that's the case, he's far enough to seek.
Poor man ! he's left us for the regions blessed,
And has in Paradise ten years confessed."

THE KISS RETURNED

A S William walking with his wife was seen,
A man of rank admired her lovely mien.
"Who gave you such a charming fair?" he cried.
"May I presume to kiss your beauteous bride?"
"With all my heart," replied the humble swain;
"You're welcome, sir;—I beg you'll not refrain.
She's at your service; take the boon, I pray;
You'll not such offers meet with every day."

The gentleman proceeded as desired;
To get a kiss alone he had aspired;
So fervently, howe'er, he pressed her lip
That Petronella blushed at every sip.

Seven days had scarcely run, when to his arms
The other took a wife with seraph charms;
And William was allowed to have a kiss,
That filled his soul with soft ecstatic bliss.
Cried he, "I wish (and truly I am grieved)
That when the gentleman a kiss received
From her I love, he'd gone to greater height,
And with my Petronella passed the night."

SISTER JANE

WHILE sister Jane, who had produced a child,
In prayer and penance all her hours beguiled,
Her sister-nuns around the lattice pressed ;
On which the abbess thus her flock addressed :
" Live like our sister Jane, and bid adieu
To worldly cares ;—have better things in view."

" Yes," they replied, " we sage like her shall be
When we with love have equally been free."

AN IMITATION OF ANACREON

PAINTER in Paphos and Cythera famed,
   Depict, I pray, the absent Iris' face.
      Thou hast not seen the lovely nymph I've named—
The better for thy peace.   Then will I trace
For thy instruction her transcendent grace.
Begin with lily white and blushing rose,
Take then the Loves and Graces. . . . But what good
Words, idle words?   For Beauty's goddess could
By Iris be replaced, nor one suppose
The secret fraud—their grace so equal shows.
Thou at Cythera couldst, at Paphos too,
Of the same Iris, Venus form anew.

ANOTHER IMITATION OF
ANACREON

PRONE on my couch I calmly slept,
    Against my wont.   A little child
    Awoke me as he gently crept
And beat my door.   A tempest wild
Was raging—dark and cold the night.
" Have pity on my naked plight,"
He begged, "and ope thy door."   "Thy name ? "
I asked, admitting him.   " The same
Anon I'll tell, but first must dry
My weary limbs, then let me try
My moistened bow."   Despite my fear,
The hearth I lit, then drew me near
My guest and chafed his fingers cold.
"Why fear ?" I thought.   " Let me be bold ;
No Polyphemus he : what harm
In such a child ?   Then I'll be calm ! "
The playful boy drew out a dart,
Shook his fair locks, and to my heart
His shaft he launched.   " Love is my name,"
He thankless cried ; " I hither came
To tame thee.   In thine ardent pain
Of Cupid think and young Climene."

"Ah! now I know thee, little scamp,
Ungrateful, cruel boy!   Decamp!"
Cupid a saucy caper cut,
Skipped through the door, and as it shut,
"My bow," he taunting cried, "is sound;
Thy heart, poor comrade, feels the wound.'

END OF VOL. I.